A
short
book
about
LOVE

# A
# short
# book
# about
# LOVE

# Nicholas Murray

**seren**

seren is the book imprint of
Poetry Wales Press Ltd
Nolton Street, Bridgend, CF31 3BN, Wales
www.seren-books.com

ISBN 1-85411-303-8

A CIP record for this title is available from
the British Library

Cover photograph: Rachel Kevern

*The publisher works with the financial assistance of the
Arts Council of Wales*

Printed in Plantin by Bail & Bain Ltd, Glasgow

NOVEL: A small tale, generally of love.
Samuel Johnson
*A Dictionary of the English Language*

# 1. OBJECTS

AN ENGLISHMAN WRITES about love to the sound of Gallic laughter.

Propped on a bank of pillows, in a long white shirt and a crumpled calico nightcap, a forlorn character mimics the scowl of Ebenezer Scrooge. Mice scamper behind the wainscot and he looks out on the white sea of his coverlet, cold and disconsolate. Two further details (for the art of caricature demands a broad, well-loaded brush): an icy wind blows through ill-fitting windows, making the curtains ripple softly, and a candle flame – flattened in the unwelcome draught – casts an eery sepulchral light into the bedchamber. This is not – is it? – conducive to the pleasures of the flesh.

The English newspapers (divided, like the nation's schools, residential districts, railway carriages, by the plaited crimson rope of class distinction) are classified by size. The oblong papers, which certain old-fashioned readers persist against all the evidence in describing as 'the quality papers', are distinguished by geometry from the small square papers with red mastheads and large headlines whose subject matter seems almost wholly sexual. The gloomy sleeper, mounted on his high, cold bed, shakes out a gazette of public lubricity. He reads, in furtive silence, of the manifold occurrences of a sexual act his paper denotes as 'bonking'. In the language of the school playground he reads of 'adult scenes'. He reads also of 'nights of love', 'love rats', 'love pests', and 'love nests', but his object of study is not love. It is bonking.

Perhaps, therefore, a nation pre-occupied with other people's couplings might permit – simply by way of a change – an excursion into the wider spaces of the human heart.

Not that one would care to produce a definition of The Great Abstraction in either its upper case or its lower case versions. The poets and artists have sometimes sought to represent a podgy Cupid with a quiver of troublesome arrows and a skimpy loincloth (or less), as if love were martial and its motions threatening like a poisoned dart.

You cannot taste it, feel it, hear it, see it, smell it. It is above and beyond the reach of logic or of science. But it has objects: person, place, thing.

One might object to being called a love object – though each of us has been one at some time, because Love (let's try out the upper case version) is democratic. It brings us all down – or up. It falls for a face, a strand of hair, a certain way of walking down the street. Even the tyrant and the well-fortified misanthrope, the ugly and the cruel, the selfish and the mad, can receive a visit at any time, can be brought down – or up.

But perhaps it is necessary to look at an example.

## 2. AN EXAMPLE

THE BOY LOOKED down at the books spread out on the brown velveteen cloth which covered the stout old-fashioned table and his eyes swam with incomprehension. Tables of trigonometry, in a little book whose green cover was soft with age and much fingering, defied him, knotted his brain like a clenched fist. Outside, the rain trickled down the cast-iron drain-pipes into the yard. The table was square though it contained an apparatus underneath, stiff and squeaking, a black threaded iron bar to which a handle was connected and turned to open the jaws of the plain, scrubbed deal table-top. Into the resulting gap two leaves were slotted. The square was now an oblong. Geometry. It stood on plump, fluted legs which ended in tiny brass castors that squeaked on the dull red quarry tiles of the floor.

The boy looked again at the implacable columns of figures, arrayed like a merciless army marching on a mission of cruel retribution. None of it made sense. The more he looked, the more he despaired and slowly his eyes filled with tears. Then the old-fashioned latch on the door rattled and the boy's father came into the room, wrapped in a thick cardigan for its was a cold, damp day. He looked down at the blank page of the exercise book and saw the tears running down the boy's cheek, tears of incomprehension and despair, rehearsals (he would not yet know) for later tears. He went down on his knees and put his arms around the boy, touching his hair with the side of his own head, telling him not to despair but to run out into the garden now that the rain had stopped. Later, he would look at the figures again and they would start to make sense.

Years later, on the top deck of a red Routemaster bus, becalmed in traffic in Camden High Street, the boy – who of course was now no longer a boy but a man, who had nearly reached his father's age on that rainy day – looked out of the window, rubbing a space in the misted glass. He saw a small boy with a rucksack of books and he remembered his father's gesture, the unexpected tenderness of the stern parent, and understood for the first time that this was love.

# 3. THE PLOT THICKENS

A CONSTANT APPREHENSION of the oblong newspapers is that writers may approach the public with a disregard for the proprieties – by which they mean novels written in such a way as to cross the empty space of possibility on the firm cantilever bridge of plot. They have in mind a beginning, a middle, and an end. They are accustomed to deplore what they have heard described as the *ludic* – a suspect behaviour probably practised by foreigners, a stratagem designed to leave the sturdy Englishman, with his thick tweed jacket of hairy common sense, plotless and confused. The more conscientious explorers of the highways and byways of their newspapers (a stalled commuter train at Hayward's Heath necessitating spending rather longer than usual on the habitually-skimped arts pages) have become aware of a new term: postmodernist. They are baffled by it (but no more baffled than those whose professional task is to write sentences in which it occurs, even as they know that part of its peculiar charm is that it can be used in almost any case). The question is put (the train has now lurched forward again in the direction of East Croydon) in the following terms: can't we have some action? An unexplained corpse, a smoking pistol, a car chase, a mysterious figure in the soft shadows beneath the single street lamp, pertinent questions asked by a police inspector in the shrubbery.

One reply might be that this is the sort of thing a crumpled commuter might watch on the TV on any night of the week. But the suspicion remains that the foreigner has designs on the good sense of the decent Englishman. The names of his writers are odd and often difficult to pronounce (Nabokov, Borges, Perec) or suggestive of great effort (Proust – ah, Proust and his goddam Maman!). Why should these folk come up the garden path to poke us in the eye with a burnt stick? Why do they strew obstacles in our way? Should we have to *work* at a book? All this talk of art makes me reach for my *Radio Times*.

# 4. A PLOT

EARLY ONE SUNDAY morning, Mrs Mary Todhunter, on her way to the corner shop to purchase a pint of milk and a copy of *The News of the World*, saw the stiff, cold limb of a youthful corpse protruding from the bucket of a yellow dumper truck parked for the weekend on a piece of waste land...

[This is beginning to sound like something that has begun and that might proceed to a conclusion over the hump-backed bridge of a middle.]

You may have read of the Lambeth Dumper Truck Murders. Working late one Saturday afternoon in a converted warehouse, the three teenagers sat at their angled drawing boards, finishing, on overtime, a rushed job. Angela – for we ought to give her a name – and Tim (ditto) were in love. But Steve (ditto) was also in the room. What happened between the three of them on that spring afternoon in that deserted warehouse with its quiet telephones, cold cups of coffee, stacked blackbags of rubbish, and bright, thin tubes of light will never be known. What came out in court seemed not to be the whole story. Steve, dragged off to a prison van in which would be swallowed up his youth, screamed to the jurors that he was innocent, as killers are prone to do. It is also a habit of the guiltless. The story, as the newspapers saw it (and of course, given the element of youth, beauty and tragedy, the rag just mentioned – with its boast that all human life pressed into its up-and-down columns – was among the most prominent) was as follows. Jealous of the comely young lovers, eaten away with lust/frustrated passion, Steve had attacked them both as they giggled and canoodled at their drawing-boards, plunging his knife into the neck of sexy Tim, silencing in the same way Angela when she would not stop screaming. In the dead of night – this was the most baffling feature of the story but fact may take certain liberties denied to the practitioner of fiction – Steve had wheeled, unseen, the bodies of the teenagers, entwined in death like the Lovers of Teruel, in a wheelbarrow that had conveniently sat to hand in the mess of the yard at the back of the warehouse, along the silent streets to the piece of waste ground. Their beautiful bodies had slithered into the dirty mouth of the dumper truck where they were covered in plastic sheeting. A riffle of wind in the night, the attentions of a down-and-out fossicking for scraps of anything inter-esting, a local hound, had uncovered a disordered limb, thus preparing Mrs Mary Todhunter's near-fatal (if she was to be believed) Sunday morning shock. It was quiet on Sunday mornings in those city streets just south of the Thames, and few took any notice when the fluttering police tapes went up around the waste ground and people in white paper suits and wellingtons arrived on the scene.

But now a police siren could be heard in the direction of Mayflower Heights in Bermondsey where, on the sixteenth floor, Steve, red-eyed and feverish after a sleepless night, looked down on the snaking river and wished that the windows were not sealed to prevent his hurling himself down to the empty street below where two policemen were adjusting their hats before walking between two tall grey rubbish-cylinders to the waiting lift.

# 5. BUT WILL IT LAST?

IN THE BLACK Triplex grate the coals glowed, heating the back boiler, throwing out warmth into the room. In front of the fire a dishcloth hung to dry on the brass fireguard. The father sat on a comfortable chair and the two children climbed on to either knee where he rocked them gently. As they clung to him he chanted softly: 'Will you love me till I'm fifty dead? Will you love me till I'm fifty dead?' They nodded their heads. At the far end of the room the mother opened the kitchen cupboard. Its catch made a little squeak. She took out a packet of flour and shook its contents into a sieve. There was music on the wireless.

*Will you love me till I'm fifty dead?*

# 6. THE LOVE OF PLACE

THE LITTLE TOWN can be approached in two ways. You may take one of the long, low, dirty yellow hydrofoils from Athens known as the Flying Dolphin. Stopping at various islands, it moves down the eastern coast of the Peloponnese, making brief stops at little harbours where, shedding momentum, it sinks down to the level of a mere caique and glides in to the quay. It does not waste time. Within minutes of landing its engines roar as it sweeps out again into the open sea. The other way of approaching the town is by bus. This involves a change at Argos where the citadel looks down on the city, on its pleasant paved *plateias* and enormous market square where once a week the country people come in to sell their produce under awnings erected the night before: great glossy aubergines, bowls of glistening olives, plastic bottles of home-pressed olive oil and home-made wine, mounds of wilting green herbs (parsley, dill and coriander), pyramids of tomatoes, oranges, apples and pears, thick ribbed green peppers, and globe artichokes. Under cover, along one side of the square, bright lamps shine on the stalls of the meat market and the sluiced fish-stalls. All the cafés are full. The old men sip their little white cups of coffee and the gypsy children flounce past with plastic novelties, demanding money with careless grace, affecting indifference to whether or not a purchase is made.

From a quiet square the bus leaves for the town. It is a pleasant journey along twisting roads high above the rugged coast with glimpses of blue sea and perfect beaches. The bus deposits you in the centre of town from where you must walk out across the stone bridge above the dried-up river bed. The road runs between rows of flaking eucalyptus for three or four kilometres, passing intensely cultivated fields of aubergine and courgette, silvery, rustling olive groves under whose shade a donkey might be tethered. Carefully constructed irrigation channels divide the fields neatly into geometric patterns. It is hot on the tarmac road and the prospect of a plunge into the sea becomes more and more enticing. Eventually the little port is reached with its tavernas and rooms for rent. Perhaps there is a vacancy at the blue and white hotel which seems to be built on the beach itself where the waves are sucking back the rounded pebbles in preparation for casting them back up again on the shelving bank. Along the waterfront a few fishermen are patching yellow nets. A trickle of fresh water runs into the sea, encouraging a small platoon of ducks to float around this tiny tributary – or perhaps to waddle along the front in search of scraps of bread thrown by the idlers on the restaurant terrace.

When it is cooler, you walk back along the road to explore the town, noting with regret that the little bakery in a side street which sold syrupy cakes and cold milk is closed since your last visit. It is a town that has not laid itself out before the foreigners, who come in small numbers. It is perhaps keeping the secret of itself, a place where the Greeks themselves like to come for long weekends and summer breaks from the stifling air, traffic roar and ugly *nefos* of Athens. Those refurbished houses along the road with their balconies and walled-off gardens are owned not by people from the cold parts of northern Europe but by rich Athenians or businessmen from Nauplion. At the far end of town the restaurant is also gone where the fat proprietor stood, announcing to the occasional foreign visitor that he had spent twenty years in Cincinnati, Ohio.

It was to here one night that the musicians came, with a violin, a clarinet, a boy with a tin plate to collect coins. In the corner, the gibes of three men sharing a forked salad offended the musicians who stopped their playing abruptly, snapped shut the violin case, and went out into the warm night. Later, the sound of their playing at a café at the other end of town attracted a small crowd. The clarinettist, with his shrieking horn and his mad priapic dance, followed the boy as the coins clattered on to the plate, wooing at each table the drinkers and the old men swinging their amber worry-beads, pleasing the entranced foreigners who had seen nothing like it before but whose hands dared not stray to their camera-bags.

Places change. They stay the same. They are in process. They can be as haunting, as insistent as the face of a loved one. They can exasperate and they can console. They are the sites of our younger selves and their escapades and encounters. They are the places where we loved or suffered or fought. They can call to us down the long corridors of memory and desire.

*Will you love me till I'm fifty dead? Will you love me till I'm fifty dead?*

# 7. WHEN DID IT BEGIN?

LOVERS AMUSE THEMSELVES in trying to settle the question of when it began. *When did we first meet?* Oddly, accounts conflict. Shouldn't this be easy? Shouldn't the moment be etched into the hard metal of memory? Is the earth not scorched here where the explosion took place? The bark scratched and the lower branches ripped and split where the speeding car left the road? But the science of love is not forensic. Let us demolish a romantic commonplace which has the lovers enact a simultaneous rapture, an exactly coterminous leap of two hearts. The poets (of whom more later) have always traded in this conceit. Likewise the multiple authors of those pocket-sized romances which are displayed near the supermarket checkout and which are later sold in bargain bundles of twenty, bound like asparagus spears, in the charity shops. But this presupposes the equal preparedness of two minds and hearts. Yet the human heart, quite apart from the human mind, is not an easily governable thing. You would agree? To arrange an event like the falling apart of a crisp apple halved by a swift knife-blow, the two parts hardly yet able to forget their conjunction, is little short of miraculous.

But then love might be considered a miracle. Yet even the incurable romantic – when writing of love – might be allowed to try for a little in the way of precision. Keats, it will be remembered, wrote:

> *Do not all charms fly*
> *At the mere touch of cold philosophy.*

But what's wrong with trying to get it right? After all, lovers generally act as though what they have is the only thing that matters. Which is rather how philosophers regard their pursuit of Truth. (Though one would want to exercise caution over anything that comes wearing an initial capital.)

Like a waiting passenger at a country halt, screwing up her eyes to see if the train is coming. Is that an illusion? Is that tiny dot, where the parallel lines seem to the eye to converge, the slowly materialising yellow face of a Sprinter train? No. Yes, that's it alright. Once it's glimpsed the doubt vanishes.

I see her in a large open foyer, her long skirt sweeping the ground. Her laughter, her curls... But she sees it, perhaps, rather differently. Another time and place, another gesture. Perhaps the mind deceives us.

Which wouldn't be for the first time.

Perhaps it chooses to reconstruct the history it wants, that fits the trajectory of its desire. I like this story. This is the narrative that takes me where I want to go. Your narrative is different. Like families puzzled by their several versions of their own history. Did he really see it like this? Did she think that is how it happened? How could he? How could she? *That's not how I remember it!*

# 8. AN INTERVENTION

'SORRY TO BUTT in, guys, but isn't this discussion a trifle, well, *masculine?*'

'Trish!'

'You see, I'm not sure we're all on the same page. Or maybe yours is Byron's: *Man's love is is of man's life a thing apart/'Tis woman's whole existence.*'

'The point being?'

'That men consider love to be a something that they indulge in from time to time but it musn't get in the way of beating their hairy chests, swinging from trees, emoting in the woods, making money, doing business, dismantling cars, being generally *macho*. Whereas we women, poor things, make it our only concern. We take it too seriously. We sit at home and weep, unpicking yesterday's work at the loom, starting again in the morning. Dogged, pathetic, whingey.'

'Not how I had you down, Trish.'

'Too right you didn't!'

'Men and women will see love differently. Sometimes they will see it in the same way. They will quarrel, they will embrace. He will idealise and so will she. Both will be cynical, disappointed, unillusioned. Or elated, dreamy, hopeful, enchanted. They will say: 'Men!' or 'Women!' but love will alter their script from time to time.'

'I think we will come back to this.'

# 9. MORE STORIES

THE JURORS BEGAN their second day at the Central Criminal Court in the expectation of more time-wasting. More long, inconsequential vigils outside courts which, in the end, turned out not to need them. They had spent most of the first day in the canteen, consuming multiple cups of tea and getting to know each other (the man who painted military models, the anxious teacher, the aloof mature student reading a slim volume of verse, the noisy little platoon of tabloid readers whose rolled-up newspapers with red mastheads and enormous headlines, tapped on the knee for emphasis, had signalled their inevitable sodality). Eventually, just after three in the afternoon, they were sent home. Tuesday morning seemed to promise more of the same but, at 9.33 am precisely, an officious middle-aged woman marched up to them to say that they were wanted at Court Number One.

In the court, a tiny judge – later they would joke that he was perched on a mound of soft velvet cushions – sat beneath a sword which, so the officious woman had informed them, indicated that he was the most senior judge in session that day. The jury settled into their places and, rather quickly, the prisoner emerged from the bowel of the panelled court to plead, without emotion, not guilty to murder. 'Murder,' each of the twelve murmured inwardly. 'That's a bit more like it.'

The prisoner was a lanky, pale-faced young man in his late twenties who displayed almost no emotion for the next two days. Some of the jurors were disappointed. Surely a murderer should look a bit evil or slyly dishonest – perhaps even remorseful? The barristers (whose voices were plummy in order that they might be distinguished from the prisoner and from the sequence of witnesses who spoke like the café proprietors outside in Old Bailey) fell to work. It seemed, from one point of view, an open-and-shut case. There was no doubt that the prisoner had done the deed. It was rather a question of establishing a motive and determining the degree of culpability. Well before lunch, the motive took the stand. He was shorter and plumper than the lanky homicide and his lightly-worn charm pronounced that he was Jack-the-lad. The jury (it was rather early in the morning for this sort of thing) had already taken from the brown envelopes in front of them the photograph of her slender, naked body punctured with a dozen horrible wounds, lying on a slab at the police mortuary. They had looked up at Passionless Pete (the title later awarded by the jury room's inevitable wag) and asked themselves what sort of relationship the two had enjoyed and why it had come to this. Jack-the-lad, trying not to smirk, was, it turned out, the best friend who had seen just as much of that long, slim body as the pathologist or the police photographer, except that it had been very much alive at the time.

The court had decided, as the most economical way of proceeding, to represent the deceased as a tart. After all, she was not now in a position to answer back. Exercising her sexual allure, she had enticed the reluctant Jack into bed while Pete was out attending to a telephone fault in Upper Norwood. Jack agreed with the barrister's gently enforced implication that he had done no more than any normal red-blooded male would have done. 'So,' counsel concluded, hitching up his robe in the process, 'she set her cap at you?' Jack smiled in place of understanding. At least half the jury tried to think when they had last heard, or read, such a phrase. Trollope? Jane Austen? The other half would have been quite as perplexed – had the exchange of smirks between the garage mechanic and the QC not made every-thing abundantly clear.

Having established the shameless hussy's unbearable provocation, a quick canter through the events of the night of the murder was required. The usher brought to the jury a repulsive tray of bloody kitchen knives under a film of tightly-stretched polythene. After some lame inquiries by the defence as to why this array of murderous kitchen equipment just happened to be in the bedroom when the victim arrived home on her last night, late and tipsy, the trial moved swiftly to its conclusion. The tiny judge, in his prim summing-up, called the victim 'wanton' (Henry Fielding? Max Beerbohm?), reminded the jury that she was no better than she ought to be, and urged them to retire. After forty uncomfortable minutes, they returned with a verdict of manslaughter but gasped with disbelief when the judge pronounced sentence of only two years. They filed slowly out, thinking of those gaping wounds, of those men in wigs pronouncing her a tart, of the quiet horror that the court had walked carefully around. Then the anxious teacher said what they had really not wanted to hear: 'But he *killed* her!'

'An extreme example of the sort of violence towards women we see every...'

'Trish, no-one is disputing that.'

'But why does it go on happening? Why do men hate women even as they pretend to be loving them? Why does love so often end like this?'

'I hope you weren't expecting any answers.'

# 10. OSCAR THE HOUND

IT WAS JUST before lunch on the Sunday before Christmas when the boy was sent by his father on an errand. He had been up early to serve Mass and he was looking forward to his lunch. The Corkerys lived in a semi-detached house with a pleasant bow-window in a cul-de-sac a mile away. Leaning his bicycle against the outside wall, he pressed the bell and Mrs Quigly came to the door. She was the elder of the two sisters, both of whom rather alarmed the boy. In their reckless generosity there was a hint of menace, as if something was being exacted at the point of giving, as if their bony fingers were finding some purchase on the recipient, as if, in some obscure way, he had not heard the last of this.

Mrs Quigly had been (in the days before her fate was briefly entwined with that of the vanished Mr Quigly) a steward on the Cunard boats. She had been to America many times but life on the ships had been no picnic. Not for the first time the boy was reminded how hard the world could be, setting its face against you like a brutal history master, constantly searching for new ways to show how cruel it was possible to be. She had told him before how the young girls would have to tip the chefs in the kitchen before they could load up their trays, hoping to recoup the loss with their own tips in the saloon. Their quarters had been cramped, their hours long, and their wages low. But they had seen New York. They had looked up at the skyscrapers, drunk steaming coffee at street stalls, and brought home presents for their family. They had gone to the pictures, watched the racing words of the circulating neon news bulletins in Times Square, and soaked up the sounds and sights of another world. But the boy was told none of this. He knew only the stories of hardship, injustice, and strife.

Mrs Quigly led him into the front room where her sister, Mrs Mason, was sitting – her trailing right hand stroking a large plump black labrador, her left clutching to her breast a thick bottomed glass of whisky. The table was set up and their brother, Frank Corkery, had just started to carve a roast joint. He smiled at the boy a little stiffly then returned to his task. He agitated the carving knife vigorously against the cold steel sharpener – both implements gripped by angular bone handles – then sliced the string which bound the meat before starting to saw off thick juicy pieces of beef. Mrs Mason, the boy had once heard other adults say, was a grass widow. There had also been some talk of a ring 'tossed from the Irish boat'. There seemed, to the boy, something sinister in the hissing, sibilant sound of 'grass widow', something malign slithering away into the dry undergrowth. He was frightened of Mrs Mason even as she reached over to the glass cabinet and took out a cylindrical tin of salted peanuts. He stepped forward to accept his reward. Mrs Mason then handed him a parcel, wrapped in Christmas paper, telling him to take care on his bicycle not to let it drop. Mrs Quigly looked on and smiled when his father was mentioned. They had also known his grandfather, the barber, in the days when they were little girls running around the streets that led down to the cobbles and massive walls of the Dock Road. Mrs Quigly came close to the boy and put her hand on his shoulder. He was terrified of her wrinkled, bony, right hand for there was a finger missing from an accident many years ago. It was horrible to look at – just a pucker of badly sewn-up skin. He dreaded being touched by it. But she continued to gaze on him, smiling.

'Felix,' she said. 'Your grandfather was the last man to shave my father before he died.'

Frank looked up from his carving and smiled. Mrs Mason smiled and stroked the big black labrador, Oscar, in his absurd little knitted red wool coat. The dog stirred and licked his lips with the sweep of a long pink tongue. He looked haughtily at Felix. He was dopey and overfed and the two women loved him, as they loved their brother – for there was no-one left in their bitter lives to love. The dog seemed grateful for this constant stream of luxury and solicitation, but there was a look of perplexity in his eye. Grateful to have fallen on such good times, Oscar could not quite understand his luck or why he had been selected by these indulgent women as the recipient of their largesse. Stretching out his paws, he closed his eyes and slept.

Felix said it was time to go. Frank lifted the carving knife and held it mockingly in front of his face in salute, like the sword of a Household Cavalryman, and smiled again. The boy closed the door behind him and strapped the parcel into his saddle-bag. As he pedalled through the suburban streets he thought of the ring, hurled angrily from the rail and finding its way, many weeks later, to the mucky foreshore where some beachcomber in a long green mac would seize on it with delight.

# 11. FELIX

FELIX, THE HAPPY or fortunate one.

Yes, but for how long? Let's settle for the end of the day. Let's not be unreasonable. One doesn't want, in all conscience, to push one's luck.

Adolescent philosophers, late night talkers in student digs, will debate the purpose of life. Later, they will discover it has none, except to realise itself. To live well, at the fullest reach of one's faculties, is all one can hope for. But to have been touched at some point by love, to have known it, however briefly, is something. It is more than something. It may be everything. Writers have reached much the same conclusion about their art. 'Poetry,' wrote Wallace Stevens, 'is a response to the daily necessity of getting the world right.' A baker in the early morning, catching the sweet smell from an oven of loaves, might be disposed to agree. That odd, engaging, Frenchman, Georges Perec, put it like this: 'To write: to try meticulously to retain something, to cause something to survive; to wrest a few precise scraps from the void as it grows, to leave somewhere a furrow, a trace, a mark, or a few signs.' I like that: *a few precise scraps.* That will do very well.

There are those who declare (in triumph) that they are on the side of Life. Dropping their usual objection to a concept that comes in the livery of an initial capital, they assert their belief in the value of actual and continuing existence. Life is a rough business (they continue). Yet all you fancy writers can do is to sit at your desks weaving patterns with words while life goes on outside in the street.

But surely (the writer objects) art is life? In the shocked silence that follows, he seizes his opportunity:

I've always been amused by the obsession of middle-class intellectuals with 'the street'. I've always regarded it as a rather functional thoroughfare, something that takes me from A to B. Joyce (realising that the ivory tower is built not by the icily superior artist but by the grinning populist who eagerly scoops out the moat that will exclude him from its mossy approach) put it this way: 'that is the great mistake everyone makes. Art is not an escape from life!' His protagonist Stephen Dedalus had a great deal to say on this question. Another quotation: 'For Stephen art was neither a copy nor an imitation of nature: the artistic process was a natural process.' You see, writing is like life in that it has no end but itself – with the exception of cookery books and instruction manuals of course. You will now ask why one does something that appears to lack immediate utility. It is a good question and one that occurred to Virginia Woolf at the end of May, 1933. It was something she wrote in a notebook about how it seems to mean everything and nothing at the same time: 'I thought, driving through Richmond last night, something very profound about the synthesis of my being: how only writing composes it: how nothing makes a whole unless I am writing; now I have forgotten what seemed so profound.'

Felix was in love. It was an element in which he moved, discreetly. It did not protect him from the sharp edges and rebuffs of life. It was not an escape, as Joyce insisted Art was not an escape. It was not continuous or histrionic ecstasy as it might be in the pages of a romantic novelist, dictating a short tale to a shorthand typist in her pink boudoir. It was not smug or pleased with itself or over-confident of its durability, or the launch-pad for extravagant philosophical claims, but it was there like a faint musical score heard along a softly-carpeted corridor in mid-morning in a concert hall where an orchestra was rehearsing. It was enough to say that it existed.

His father was fond of light verse and nonsense. Felix grew up surrounded by the vivacity of neat rhymes and sprightly nothings. He swam in a pool of jokes, some of which, as is often the case with jokes, would not seem so funny if repeated here. At one point he thought *The Walrus and the Carpenter* the equal of *Lycidas*. In a city of jokers and wits, his father was a joker and wit, who could also be fierce and angry when the world hurt him, as it sometimes did, but who never stopped making jokes. Felix once visited him in hospital, where he clung pitifully on a hot June day to a thick-ribbed radiator. He was in the wing of the building that had once been the old workhouse. His father's great aunt – a feckless toper – had died there at the end of the last century. Felix looked at his shivering father, who was in great pain but who was struggling to let a confined and cramped joke out into the stuffy air of the ward: 'I never thought I would end my days in the workhouse.' Ha! Ha! Felix went out into the street to catch a green double-decker bus. It was raining hard and the sloshing water that threw itself against the windows of the bus trickled down like tears.

> *They wept like anything to see*
> *Such quantities of sand.*

Felix had many uncles who were also in love, in love with jokes. Uncle Dermot, the science teacher, was rumoured to have a camp-bed at the back of the lab where he would take a quick nap while the pupils wiggled their test tubes in the blue flames of the Bunsen burner. When teachers' salaries were newly structured by a man called Burnham, Uncle Dermot went down to his friend, Harry Diggle, the wood-work teacher, and borrowed a piece of two-by-two. He marked it with a series of notches then placed it in the ground where it was visible from the staff-room window. He brought his colleagues away from their exercise books, their pipes, their crosswords, and their cups of tea. 'That's my graded post,' he announced with a chuckle.

> *The Carpenter said nothing but*
> *'Cut us another slice'*

And there was Uncle Mick who had known some music hall artists in the War. On Christmas Day, after the tables had been cleared and the adults were topping up their whisky in the front room, he would entertain Felix and his brother and sister and his cousins (who together made quite a crowd) in front of the gas fire in the back room. They whooped and hooted with laughter as Uncle Mick started to sew his fingers together in a mime. Sometimes Uncle Dermot would come in and start to tell some of his docker jokes. Did you hear the one about the docker they called Stanley Matthews? When a crate was lowered to the quay-side by a crane he would always be the first to shout: 'I'll take this corner!'

Why were these men so addicted to jokes?

> *But answer came there none.*

# 12. THE REAL WORLD

WE HAVE PUT the old century behind us. Perhaps it has tired us all out. Perhaps that is why the utopians and dreamers and architects of new worlds – of better worlds – have given up. Their blueprints and manifestos and schemes and projections are heaped up like old cars in a scrap yard. Look at that blue Ford, perched precariously on the top of the heap, rocking gently, put there as a joke by the scrap metal men. Shall we call it Socialism?

Ivan Mishukov is a real boy in a real city. I have not made him up. The municipality of Reutova, west of Moscow, is very angry with Ivan Mishukov, and with the world's media. For they have told the story of Ivan Mishukov, who (two years before the century finally ended, before it finally called it a day) lived wild with a pack of dogs. From the age of four until the age of six Ivan had run with the pack after having been abandoned by his parents. He feared the brutality of the crowded orphanage and he lived – in a city where the winter temperatures fall to 30 degrees below zero – on rubbish tips, sewers next to underground hot water pipes, cellars and attics in disused buildings. In Russia, where the machinery of Socialism rusts in an untidy heap, there were two million homeless children in the last year of Ivan's life amongst his animal friends. Two hundred were killed by their parents, 17,000 attempts were made on the lives of children, and ten per cent of children turned out of orphanages to fend for themselves committed suicide. That is enough statistics. That is quite enough numbers.

The police had some difficulty in catching Ivan Mishukov. The dogs were fiercely protective of their companion. After three separate attempts, the police set a bait of meat inside the storage room of a restaurant where the dogs would come at night to forage for leftovers. They slammed the doors shut and dragged away the howling, biting child from his friends.

His body crawling with lice and broken with sores, six-year-old Ivan Mishukov told the police: 'I was better off with the dogs. They loved and protected me.'

## 13. THE DINNER JACKET

FELIX WAS WALKING along the street with his father when an old man approached, grave and unsmiling. He wore a long black overcoat and a soft black hat. The two men greeted each other warmly and the old man looked down with brief interest at the boy. Nathan Gombrich had seven sons, each of whom was a doctor of medicine. Years ago the Gombriches had won a contest against the family of Felix's father. They had won it hands down. In the cobbled street where the barber's shop was situated, not far from the music hall (now a discount carpet store) where his father would lie awake on Saturday nights hearing the roar of: 'Yes! We have no bananas!', the arrival of the Gombriches put paid to the supremacy of the family of Felix's father. No longer were they the poorest family in the street – though never the glummest, as their songs and jokes would testify – displaced overnight by a Polish tailor and his swelling family. Long afterwards, long after his official retirement, Nathan would continue to make suits for Felix's father and for his many uncles. They were thick, heavy suits with waistcoats and buttons in all the right places and with buttonholes for wedding-morning white flower sprays, and with generous lapels. No corners were cut by this ancient cutter in his long, dark coat.

Much later, Felix would remember Nathan Gombrich and his seven sons, on a morning when he swished the contents of his wardrobe in panic, looking for an ironed shirt, and saw, hanging at the end of the row, the heavy dinner jacket with its sharp, dashing lapels and its superfluity of black buttons. He lifted out the heavy suit, which the frail wire coat hanger seemed barely able to sustain, and looked on Nathan's handiwork. He slipped his hand into the deep pocket and pulled out a black tie with its trailing ribbon. And then he saw his father, Brylcreemed and alert, taking his mother's arm in her long red ballgown, on one of those rare nights when they swept out to a dance in a flourish of fur stoles and shiny patent leather shoes.

Could he put it on? Could he carry it off? Or should it remain in the dark interior of the wardrobe, straining the hanger out of shape, gathering a patina of gentle dust?

# 14. THE GREAT LOVE STORIES

'HOW ON EARTH,' Virginia Woolf asked Ethel Smyth in 1938, 'does one explain madness and love in sober prose, with dates attached.' There are no dates attached to the love of Tristan and Iseut because the legend bubbles up, as legends do, from nowhere in particular. The songs the *jongleurs* sang and which were later written down as manuscripts by half-identified persons about whom we know nothing, were themselves adaptations, re-tellings, embroiderings of the legend. The first twelfth century manuscripts are lost – probably torn up and used as lining paper or covers for other books. Who first told the story, who got it from whom, whether Tristan and Iseut ever lived, are unanswerable questions. But this story which came from nowhere has reached everywhere. It has colonised the imagination of everyone who has heard of it. It is like a virus that cannot be resisted. It is more real than cold water or rock or the crashing of the waves, yet it may be an invention.

In the twelfth century manuscript of Thomas the Anglo-Norman (one doesn't wish to impress so let it be said that our source is a chance discovery in a charity shop in Llandrindod Wells of a little book called *Tristan in Brittany* published in 1929 by Ernest Benn of Bouverie House, Fleet Street, EC4 in Benn's Essex Library (cloth, gilt back, 3s.6d each net.) The translator was a Dorothy Leigh Sayers, 'sometime scholar of Somerville College, Oxford'). Better known, perhaps, as the creator of Lord Peter Wimsey the classy detective. Benn's Essex Library (one couldn't help noticing) was offering to the earnest autodidact of the 1920s a range of other titles including: *Climbs on Alpine Peaks*, by

His Holiness Pope Pius XI. *Rhymes of a Rolling Stone* by Robert Service. *Fundamental Thoughts in Economics* by Gustav Cassel. The roll-call of old books is a chastening thought. How few remain, like beached logs after flood-waters recede. But that's another story.

Miss Sayer's work (I rather think she would baulk at 'Ms') is supposed to be a translation of a verse romance but half of it is actually in prose. The verse is quite fast and flowing but she does tend to use bits of antique Chaucerian lingo here and there. We know nothing at all about the author Thomas (which today would be intolerable, an affront to features editors, and blurb-writers, to publicists confecting an angle) but his story lives.

Tristan, the un-Felix, was so christened by his mother who died shortly after giving birth and who, rightly as it turned out, predicted for him a life of sadness (*triste homme*). He is our example of what happens when the apple of love goes pear-shaped.

Were the story one of two happy and contented lovers the world would have lost interest several centuries ago. But this one has all the ingredients: illicit desire, madness, jealousy, deceit, sex, death, snobbery, fights, travel, historical costume (which makes one think of Sunday night TV). And magic. Not something we care to believe in now, unless it's wrapped up as newspaper horoscopes, lucky lottery numbers, New Age therapies, walking on the other side of the street, crediting miracles. In the case of Tristan we are talking love-philtres.

Tristan was born in Lyonnais, which doesn't help much because no such place exists. Think of it as out at sea, between Cornwall and the Scilly Isles, where it was said to have sunk. After various adventures (where the killing of dragons would be a mandatory element) he was sent by his protector King Mark of Cornwall to Ireland where he clapped eyes on Iseut. Iseut the Fair, not to be confused with her mother Queen Iseut of Ireland, nor Iseut of the White Hands.

On this first trip he was not smitten. But soon he was despatched once more to Ireland with the mission of bringing back Iseut as a bride for King Mark (the nobles, worried that Tristan, who was flavour of the month, might get the succession from the childless King, had set up this little match to make sure the insufferably handsome, brave, and generally faultless, outsider didn't get a look in). Queen Iseut (mother of the prospective bride) was something of a genius when it came to herbal remedies. She had already saved Tristan's life by these means and now she prepared a love-philtre. Perhaps she knew something about the potential sexual allure, for a young girl, of the Cornish bachelor-king and had decided a little help might be needed. She handed the philtre to Iseut's maid, Brangain, for safe-keeping. Stories of this kind generally demand an error that we can see coming and the mistake was duly accomplished by poor Brangain who left the flask containing the philtre next to her bunk. It was a hot, sunny voyage so Tristan sent one of his pages below deck for something to drink. You can guess what he returned with. Tristan, who was very well-mannered, poured out half for himself and half for his monarch's bride-to-be, said 'Cheers!', and quaffed it down. As the creator of Lord Peter Wimsey renders it: 'The sweet poison of love moved in their veins and tormented them, so that their tongues stammered and words came brokenly.' That was it. The two would now love without interruption for ever until their deaths, whatever calamities might be heaped upon them – and where Tristan and Iseut were concerned, calamity was their middle name.

We no longer believe in magic philtres but the *amour fou* has certainly not had its day.

# 15. THE LOVE OF GOD

FELIX WOKE TO the drumming of the alarm which at first
had seemed part of his dream but which now rang out
clearly and sharply in the real, if shadowly-defined, darkness
of the new morning. No light penetrated the curtain. The
house was quiet and still. He jumped out of bed quickly, for
the alarm had been set rather too late. He went into the bathroom and turned on the tap, splashing himself with the icy
cold water, then crept back to his room to dress. He moved
silently down the stairs and along the passage to the back
door where he slid back the bolt and stepped into the yard.
The sky was now beginning to change colour as dawn
approached. He walked swiftly across the yard to the back
door where the white rabbit in its hutch wrinkled its nose
and looked at him interrogatively. He slid back the second
bolt, this time on the back gate set in a high brick wall, and
came out into the street. He started to run because it was late
and arrived, five minutes later and out of breath, at the low
building which ran away from the church to the left. He
opened the wooden door and ran into the narrow room
behind the sacristy. Pulling off his coat, he opened the doors
of the dark, cavernous cupboard and climbed inside, quickly
searching for a black cassock that would fit. The only item
that was the right length was missing half its buttons but it
would have to do. Next he dragged open the drawer in which
the neatly ironed surplices (the loving work of the Sisters of
Mary) were stacked. Pulling one over his head, he rushed
down the tiny corridor only just in time to meet the priest as
he emerged from the sacristy. Leading the procession of two
out into the church, Felix prepared to meet the priest's

announcement at the altar steps: *Introibo ad altare dei* – I will go to the altar of God – with the proper response: *ad deum qui laetificat juventatem meam* – the God of my gladness and joy. Then he sank to his knees as the priest deposited his holy tools on the altar table and unlocked the tabernacle.

As they had passed to the altar, Felix had thrown a quick glance out into the church: a crone in a black mantilla, pale faced and ancient, leaned over her pew, with her black rosary beads dangling down before her; a man in a yellow scarf knelt three rows behind her; and in the very front row – sprawled awkwardly as a result, in equal measure, of his disability and his extravagant piety, was the wholly expected figure of Joseph Phelan. Joseph had stopped Felix in the street only three days before, apparently forgetful of an episode six months previously when he had invited the boy to his house to listen to a piece of music – the all-too-sweet fluting of some celebrated counter-tenor whose acquaintance Joseph had claimed to have made at a retreat. A fire had glowed in the open grate. An oil painting of Grandfather Phelan (a crabbed Edwardian patriarch) hung above the mantelpiece. Joseph had returned to the room, limping in that ungainly way that made everyone sorry for him, and bearing a bottle of sherry and two glasses. Sensing – with the preternatural awareness of the young – that something was not quite right in the atmosphere, Felix had jumped up abruptly to announce that he was late and really must go. The wretched man blinked behind his thick glasses, still holding the bottle of cheap sherry, and watched the boy scuttle out of the room.

*Blessed be the great Mother of God, Mary most holy.*
*Blessed be her holy and Immaculate Conception.*
*Blessed be her glorious Assumption*
*Blessed be Joseph, her spouse most chaste.*

Joseph lifted his eyes at the presentation of the Host and his body filled with the love of God as the bell tinkled in

Felix's hand.

Three days earlier, he had stopped the boy in the street.

'Felix, can you guess which is my favourite day of the week?'

'No, Mr Phelan.'

'Friday. Do you know why that is, Felix?'

'No, Mr Phelan.'

'Because it was on Good Friday that Our Lord died on the cross for our sins.'

# 16. OF THE PLEASURES
# OF THE FLESH

'AHAH!'

She took the lovely, plump, shiny aubergine and placed it before her on the chopping board. Carefully, she sliced it lengthwise into half-inch thick pieces which she then dropped into a frying-pan of hot sunflower oil. Fried on both sides, they would soften until they were ready to be lifted out and drained of their surplus oil on an unfurled sheet of paper kitchen towel. While this slow sizzling was in progress, she would peel two large onions, halve them, and slice them thinly on the board. These would be shovelled into a separate saucepan of olive oil where they would, over a low heat, soften until transparent. Shortly before they were ready she would add two garlic cloves – peeled and thinly sliced – to the pan. Then she would add a measure of oregano, a sprinkling of thyme, and a bay leaf with salt and pepper. Then a canful of tomatoes would slip into the mixture, with a small amount of tomato purée and a teaspoon of sugar. These elements – stirred and cooked slowly for perhaps only a quarter of an hour – would then be spooned – seconds after a small mound of freshly chopped broad-leaved parsley had been added to the mixture – over the aubergine slices which had now been transferred to an attractive, oval oven dish. Some Parmesan cheese was grated over the result and the dish baked for forty minutes in a medium oven. Served an hour or two later, lukewarm and succulent, her fellow diner would say:

'Ambrosia must have tasted like this.'

Perhaps there were other reasons. Perhaps the soft breeze blowing through an open window. A certain inexplicable conjunction of moment and mood. But they would always remember the night that ambrosia was served as the night when something ended and something else began.

# 17. OF PLACE

FELIX STEPPED FROM the express train on to the platform like a sailor touching *terra firma* after a long voyage during which the unceasing motion of the deck has made him long for the solidity of land. He loved the city, the draw of the metropolis. Love is blind. Love is inarticulate. Love frequently mistakes its objects. Love often makes us foolish. But love is always certain of itself. It never admits to a mistake. It never carries on a debate, never gainsays instinct. His love for the city was instinctive. But it also had its reasons.

For the young provincial the city is redemptive. To the confused, the cramped or the damaged it offers the possibility of a certain kind of freedom. A certain kind of cancellation. An opportunity to start again. It is faceless, anonymous, cold, lacking the warm certainties of neighbourhood and rooted memory. Excellent! There is nothing better than a clean sheet. The chance of a second attempt. The chance to walk unencumbered. To travel light.

'Isn't there a word you haven't mentioned?'

'Escape.'

'Precisely.'

Felix had grown to love the city, in part for what it was not, but, increasingly now, for what it offered. Or for what it seem to offer him. It had been patient. It had been prepared to wait. It even began, with a wry smile, to let him into its secrets. The secret of neighbourhood, for example, which should have been obvious. Any spot where living takes place acquires a certain style, a certain flavour. It becomes a place within a place. It claims the privileges of the gossipy village with its pride and its prejudices, its boast of community.

Felix walked out of the station, noting with approval the bright sunshine and the clear sky. There was a freshness and expectancy in the morning that he relished. He crossed the fast main road at the traffic lights and, glad now to be able to exercise his knowledge of the city, plunged sideways into an alley of little shops and restaurants. He noticed some private dwellings above them, an iron balcony, a cascading window-box. He pressed on – across a grassed square, along a curving crescent of small hotels – to the street. It contained a small baker, a wet-fish shop, a cobbler (a cobbler!), a hardware shop flaunting buckets and mops and aluminium step-ladders, a bookshop for military hobbyists, a Chinese restaurant, an Italian restaurant [he looks up to where a silver jet crosses the blue lake of sky], a community centre (whose window displayed advertisements for household items for sale, timings of councillor's surgeries, telephone numbers of advice lines), a newsagent, a pub and a chemist's shop. There were council flats in a dense concentration so it was not an exclusive neighbourhood of the rich. And the tourists, dragging suitcases on retractable wheels, trundled past an old woman on her way to buy a loaf, their city written in a different script.

Felix fitted his key into the lock of a door between an electrical shop and a launderette, picked up a fistful of mail, and climbed up the narrow stairs to the top floor flat.

# 18. THE POETS

'SPARE ME!'

'I'm sorry, Trish.'

'It may have escaped your notice but most poets appear to be male – thanks to the jiggery-pokery of the text-book writers as much as anything – and nine times out of ten the 'object' of their lyrical love is a woman.'

'Well, I suppose love is better than hate.'

'Don't try and be smart-ass, you know exactly what I mean, the woman created by these poets is either soppy and idealised or cruel and vindictive – which is another way of saying she doesn't roll over to order. One thing's for sure, she can't win either way and we never hear her side of the story.'

'Have you finished?'

'For the time being. Convince me I'm wrong.'

'For a start, if you look at the early stuff – Tristan and Iseut, for example, which I'll be coming back to later – the women are far from being drippy heroines. Iseut is quite a tough cookie. But I want to kick off with John Donne.'

'Oh, yes, the one who found a new continent under his mistress's drawers.'

'Come on, Trish, you know that's crap. Apart from the fact that he is, in the nature of things, the one who is largely doing the talking...

'My point precisely...'

'These are poems about sexual mutuality: *My face in thine eye, thine in mine appeares,/And true plaine hearts doe in the faces rest,/Where can we finde two better hemispheares/Without sharpe North, without declining West?*'

'All very charming, I must say.'

'He isn't making the woman into an 'object', he's writing about a shared experience of love, about it cutting both ways, and (unlike Shakespeare whose language is prettier but who in my view doesn't always give us the smell of the actual thing) there's a lived erotic intensity to these poems that still packs a powerful punch three centuries later.'

'Do you have to use all this *macho* terminology?'

'Take *The Anniversarie* for instance. For my money it puts its finger on the essence of sexual love: the way it possesses us entirely, cancelling time, the world...

'And the fact that the ironing needs doing and the kids collecting from school.'

'Trish! It might be an invention, a wish, a taunt thrown in the face of time, an act of defiance, but it feels real. And if you haven't felt the same thing at some time or other what has been the point of your life?'

'OK. OK.'

*All other things, to their destruction draw,*
*Only our love hath no decay;*
*This, no tomorrow hath, nor yesterday,*
*Running it never runs from us away,*
*But truly keepes his first, last, everlasting day.*

# 19. THE BROTHER

THE BROTHERS' HOUSE, its solid Victorian walls thickly painted in cream with maroon trimmings, stood apart at the edge of the school campus, signalling its difference from the new extensions and halls and science labs. Just before lessons began, the brothers would emerge, one by one, cigarettes extinguished, their black robes swirling in the breeze, a letter sometimes lodged in the broad black band around a plump midriff. They seemed, sometimes, a little sad. They reeked of stale tobacco and some spoke still in the thick brogue of their native turf. They were made fun of by the boys but they were also feared. The source of much of that fear was an object perhaps eighteen inches long and two inches wide (how to find time in the expectation of that downward swish to make one's measurements exact?). It was made from leather, thickly stitched and stiffened with whalebone. Long use made the strap supple and, in the right hands, a line of twenty boys who had forgotten the date of the Treaty of Utrecht or the exports of Brazil could be dealt with in a few minutes. One joker would enter the classroom with a strap stuck in his broad band like the six-shooter of a Wyoming gunslinger. Another swept in with a pile of exercise books, the strap laid across the top of the pile, holding the collection like a priest going up the steps to the altar with his shielded chalice. The brothers came in all shapes and sizes. They were fierce and funny. They made their pupils laugh and they made them cry. They were old and young but they were all, it seemed to the boys, lonely men whose consolation was tobacco and whatever pleasures obtained in the cream and maroon fortress of the brothers' house whose threshold no boy had ever crossed.

Can one fall in love with a spear?

The missionary took the classroom by storm. In his long white robes he talked of Africa. He was excited and alive. But his triumph was the long, carved ebony spear. Felix thought of that spear as the little squares of paper were distributed. He cast another quick glance at it as he held his pen over the paper where each boy had been instructed to write only his name and the word NO or the word YES. Because of the tall, laughing White Father. Because of the black spear, Felix wrote YES.

Next day, he was summoned from the gym to the annexe at the side of the brothers' house. He walked along the gravel walk that led to the house. This felt strange and transgressive so he was relieved when the path took a right turn away from the house towards the annexe where the White Father – who was dressed in very ordinary black now and whose spear had been put away – sat waiting for him. He waited to see if Felix had A Vocation. Perhaps it was the absence of the spear. Perhaps it was the thought of what his parents might think. Perhaps it was the thought of what a Vocation might mean. Or perhaps it was all these things. Felix looked up at the tanned missionary with the light in his eye and felt ashamed that he lacked an answering light, that he had made a mistake, that he would not now go swaggering through the jungle or race on a strongly-flowing river in a hollowed out canoe with the crew chanting a tribal song, bringing light into the darkness of the African forest. The White Father understood. He asked him to tell the next boy on the list to come. Felix ran out along the path and back to the gym where the shouts and violent rebounding of a plastic football in a furious game of five-a-side ensured that no-one would notice his re-entry.

Brother Nightingale was not like the others. Brother Nightingale had a light that burned more intently than the light in the missionary's eye. But it seemed, to the boys, the light of mania. They could not point to anything that spoke directly of madness but in the weeks leading up to would-you-believe-it? his behaviour seemed increasingly excitable. He stopped beating the boys. He forgot to set homework. He stopped talking about the Causes of the French Revolution (the Encylopaedists, Voltaire, the Ancien Régime) and talked instead about his childhood on a Wexford farm. How he had helped his father drive the cows out to pasture. The boys looked at each other nervously. What was going on? Old Nightie was off his rocker.

Would you believe it?

The news raced through the school like flame across a dry plain. He had gone. Brother Nightingale would not be back. But there was more. Each of them tried to imagine the scene. On the other side of the main road, in the Convent of the Sacred Heart of Jesus, a young nun had gone off with the crazy, jabbering, elated young brother. Neither would be back. No-one would say where they had gone. An official version was put out but the truth elbowed it roughly aside. A new history teacher – a young man in a corduroy jacket, whose real interest was sport – came to take the place of the over-excited brother whose life had been turned upside down and tossed into the air and shaken about and filled with madness and frenzy and wild, jabbering excitement and terrible confusion.

And love.

## 20. ON BEING CAREFUL

FALLING IN LOVE ought to be easy enough but the act is surrounded by pitfalls. Lovers, whose characteristic is that they don't think, would be well-advised to use a little common sense. But they are not well-advised, which is partly what love is about, and so they get into all sorts of scrapes. Tristan and Iseut would be a prime example of what happens when you don't mind your back (largely because, too often, you are on it).

Tristan discovered eventually that the dashing Romeo, the saloon-bar Lothario, the champion Latin lover, is not always wholly popular, particularly with other Romeos, Lotharios and Latins. So bad did things get in Cornwall, in fact, that he was forced to take extended leave in the court of the King of Gaul. In addition to sexual jealousy, there were those who thought he had designs on the Cornish throne. In Gaul he got mixed up with a big butch character called the Morholt who, like himself, was on a spell of leave from, in his case, Ireland. He took a good look at the Irish feller but it wasn't until some time later when he was back in Cornwall (living *incognito* for fear of stirring up more Lothario-envy and general political *angst*) that the Morholt entered his life in a big way. Try as the anonymous Tristan would, however, he couldn't prevent the young lovers and the on-message, jockeying courtiers, from resenting him. In spite of himself he was turning out to be the most handsome, most courageous, most likely of lads and was looking for an opportunity to show off. If that sounds a tad unfair it's important to remember that Tristan, in spite of always looking the part, wasn't perfect. In short, he was like the rest of us – which could be the reason why this legend has survived for eight centuries.

The Morholt, brother of Queen Iseut of Ireland (not to be confused with her daughter Iseut the Fair, nor Iseut of the White Hands) now arrived to demand tribute from Cornwall to the Irish King Anguin. This led to an outbreak of wailing and gnashing of teeth. Whingeing and whining. Confronted with this outburst of victim culture, Tristan went spare. He told the caterwauling Celts to shut up and do something about it. They looked at him in amazement. Didn't he know that the terrible Morholt was invincible? Tristan – *incognito* still – told the King that he would take on the Morholt himself if he could see his way to knighting him first. The King had no problem with this and so next day Sir Tristan as he now was pushed off in a little boat to St Samson's Isle to confront the great big Irish battleaxe.

There's no need, by the way, to look up St Samson's Isle in the Cornish gazeteer. Frankly, the geography of this tale is a bit odd but it is generally considered today that St George's Island near Looe was the battle site.

When the Morholt, who had also arrived by sea, saw Tristan cast loose his boat he was rather puzzled. Tristan explained neatly that only one man was going to leave the island alive so two boats were something of a luxury. With a grunt and a self-satisfied sneer the Morholt lifted up his club and the two went to work. The Cornish watched the whole thing from the shore where they could see the two knights hammering each other's halberks and grappling each other's greaves and, across the water, they could hear some of the grunts and howls. The Cornish fans shouted and cheered and stamped their feet like football hooligans. It wasn't a pushover for either contestant but eventually Tristan clove the Morholt's skull in two, the chopper descending as far as the Irish knight's chattering teeth. But the edge was taken from the victory by a wound Tristan had received earlier in the encounter from a poisoned lance. While the Cornish celebrated wildly, Tristan grew sicker and sicker. The medical men came forward and plastered his body with herb poultices but no-one had the wit to think of poison as the real cause of his incurable disease. Things got steadily worse until Tristan – whose wound was making such a stink few would come anywhere near him – asked for a boat rigged with a simple sail that he could steer to some country where an alternative medical knowledge might save him. Reluctantly, the Cornish let him go and after a very weepy send-off he drifted across the sea until he was washed up on the shore of Ireland. Given that he had butchered their most famous knight it was time for another *incognito*. Making some rather politically incorrect assumptions about the Irish, Tristan thought they would be fooled if he simply wrote his name backwards. He therefore announced to his new hosts that his name was Tantris.

Because of the beautiful sound of his harp the Irish hearts melted and the King, bored with endless jigs and reels, demanded to be introduced to the new virtuoso. Seeing the state he was in, he instructed his wife, Queen Iseut – or in some versions of the legend his daughter Iseut the Fair, not to be confused with Iseut of the White Hands – to apply one of her magic herbal potions to the poor suffering Tantris's wound. It drew out the poison and soon Tristan was dressing himself up in white armour and shining at the local tournament. He defeated there a knight called Palamedes, who was actually a Saracen and therefore deserved to lose. The Queen's daughter Iseut the Fair was very fair indeed and, for no reason other than to put one over on the simpering Saracen, Tristan decided to make advances to the gorgeous Iseut in spite of being, at that stage, far from smitten.

An interesting fact about the middle ages is that, far from being a smelly lot, they were actually fond of bathing. In Paris in the year 1292 there were no fewer than 26 public bath-houses. But you don't want to know this.

Bath-time seems to have been a rather festive occasion and one day Tristan was naked in the bath, surrounded by various larky members of the court and the royal family, one of whom was playing around with Tristan's sword. At this point the Queen came in, averting her eyes from Tristan's private parts (think what you like).

Seeing something odd in the great sword which had been used to kill the Morholt *viz.* a very noticeable notch in the blade, the Queen's grey matter stirred. She went into her chamber and opened a casket in which was kept a piece of Tristan's blade that had been removed from her dead brother's skull. Returning to the open-plan bathroom she fitted the piece of metal exactly into the notch on Tristan's sword. Then she started to scream blue murder:

'Tantris, my arse! This is the Tristan of Lyonnais who butchered my brother. I'll have him strung up for this!'

The Queen stormed off and demanded of the King that he execute Tristan forthwith. But the King could not get the sound of that harp out of his mind. Nor could he bring himself to chop the head off such a comely knight. In short, like everyone else, he had taken a shine to Tristan. Nonetheless, he agreed that the best thing would be for him to hop on the Irish boat and make himself scarce. Merely as a matter of prudence. In this way Tristan returned to Cornwall, his life already full of travails and upsets even before a love philtre had touched his lips.

The moral, as already noted, is that lovers should take care, or they will come unstuck. In particular they shouldn't show off or provoke the rest of us. To the fact that they will take no heed of such advice is attributable the steady flow of tragic love stories in world literature. Not to mention in real life.

# 21. LOVE UNREQUITED

THE FINAL TOUCH was a light blue silk handkerchief in the breast pocket of the suit. He looked into the mirror's depths for confirmation. He wondered, briefly, if this made him look like a Conservative MP. In the end, he decided the effect had worked. Placing on his head a brown trilby hat, he went out into the street, along the still sunny pavements, to the Underground station. The platform was empty. Two stops from the beginning – or the end – of the line, he could always be sure of a near empty carriage. As the train rattled and rumbled towards the centre of the city, soon plunging out of the sunlight into the darkness of underground, the carriages filled up with the sorts of various traveller that one sees in metro carriages across the world. They look at each other but they do not speak. Their eyes are averted. They make much use of newspapers which they read with an intentness of scrutiny that is hardly justified by their contents. They read books. They pretend to read books. They read the advertisements above the window. They fall asleep. Or they pretend to sleep. Occasionally they rise to an emotion: a look of disapproval at the young man with long legs whose V-shaped disposal of knees prevents anyone choosing the empty seats on either side of him; a frosty glance at the unsuccessful beggar passing down the carriage. There is generally little conversation. When it is clear or loud it is often in a foreign language.

It was Edward's habit to read on his journeys into work at the Institute. The reading matter had nothing to do with his work. His position was too lowly for his work to follow him out of the office. He had no pile of important-looking papers on his knee. He had no mobile phone. He was what used to be called a clerk but what was now termed a Senior Administrative Officer. He was cynical about this. On a train to Southend only the other Sunday he had said to himself in the silence that followed a fatuous announcement on the loudspeaker ('This is your Senior Conductor speaking...'): 'Do you suppose there are any Junior Conductors?' His cynicism was vital to the performance of his job. In the Institute, people like Edward were needed. People who saw through the bullshit. People who – quietly but deliberately – ensured that things happened, at the right time and in the right order. His contempt for management was absolute. Management, he believed, was a tolerated absurdity. Much of his work involved rectifying its mistakes, translating the whirling madness of its rhetoric into plain English, throwing open the large windows of good common sense so that a cold draught of fresh air swept away the foetid atmosphere of corporate blather. He had polished a series of maxims that were not his own but which he had kept in good repair and of which a representative example might be: 'Scum rises to the top.' He had worked in several organisations before settling into his present job at the Institute but each had confirmed his fundamental analysis of management: that it was generally an obstruction and that the talent in organisations – their energy and originality – lay always at the bottom where management conspired to keep it. Management, yes, was an absurdity. Life was full of such absurdities and the task of people of good sense like himself was simply to press on regardless and outwit them – which was an easy matter – in order to make happen the things that ought to happen with the minimum of fuss. In the years that he had served at the Institute, management had been infected with a new virus, a sort of restlessness, an unceasing war or Trotskyist struggle against what had been done last week, a determination that it would be done differently next week, and an

56

inability – without the aid of men such as Edward – to conduct what happened this week. There had always been a problem of language but it had got worse. Management now seemed to live entirely in a world of words and phrases that it shuffled and re-arranged like pieces on a board. It had taken flight and left reality behind – where reality was the polished mahogany cupboards containing bound volumes of the proceedings of the Institute, the sharp reek of disinfected corridors first thing on a Monday morning, the laughter from the typing pool, the crinkly sacks in the mail room, the clatter of salt cellars on the formica tables in the canteen, and the boxes of rubbish stacked outside offices with notes pinned to them announcing their need for disposal.

It was for all these reasons that Edward performed his work with extreme punctiliousness and why he left his work-place each evening at 5.25pm with a feeling of precise and cordial contempt.

His reading matter on the Underground was generally theatrical biography, showbusiness reminiscence, or books about the history of the great theatres. He occasionally ventured south of the river to the great national subsidised companies, but his heart was in the West End, in the cramped and ornate commercial theatres, with their bill-boards and their steeply-ranked seats and camp programme-sellers, and maddening pillars, and aptly-named crush bars.

And his heart was on one actress in particular.

Felicity Cazamian was, to Edward, the very model of the West End theatrical star. She had learned her trade in the theatre – her triumphs in the cinema and on television were autumnal and effortless – and had done everything and played everyone. At the age of 56 she was still – in the eyes of her unknown admirer – astonishingly beautiful. But then he had seen her only in her greasepaint and from flattering camera angles. He knew this but the fact did not worry him.

In the theatre illusion was all and no-one who could not understand the vital truth of illusion would ever comprehend its allure. As he emerged from the Underground into the bustle of the theatre district, Edward began to re-adjust himself, to prepare for the experience. He looked a little disdainfully at the scruffy crowd in its baggy jeans and T-shirts and scuffed trainers. Elegance, he reflected, was a lost art. But he was determined not to be seen as a fogey and stepped smartly into a shiny new coffee bar where he demanded an Americano. He had no idea what an Americano might be but he was determined to try. Choosing a stool against the wall he found himself examining his own reflection in a narrow, horizontal mirror. He was pleased with the result and adjusted the blue silk handkerchief. Its three crisp peaks, peeping just over the lip of the pocket, exhibited just the right amount of discreetness, of unforced style. He sipped his coffee – which turned out, in spite of all the fuss, to be a very ordinary cup of coffee – and began to anticipate his pleasure. Tickets had been more than usually difficult to obtain because Felicity was currently starring in a television series in which – Edward thought – her skills were rather underused and employed on a very inferior script. In spite of the tawdry material, however, she had done what she always did. She had shone.

Looking at his watch, Edward decided it was time to leave and to make his way along the narrow alley in the direction of the theatre. He always timed his entrance for when a crowd had gathered outside and when the foyer was full of people. He enjoyed weaving his way with elegant courtesy through the crowd, smiling as someone stood back to let him pass, accepting apologies with perfect grace, his movements lithe and practised, without a hint of clumsiness. He bought a programme and presented his ticket to the usher who showed him to his seat. It had been a wicked extravagance. The third row of the stalls, almost in the centre of the row. It had cost and arm and a leg but Edward would have sacrificed all four limbs for an unimpeded view of Felicity Cazamian.

The play was a new one and on four occasions Edward winced at the bad language which seemed – he was afraid – gratuitous. But Felicity did not let him down. Her performance was exquisite and she had some marvellous lines to deliver – even to this cackling audience of tourists and corporate hospitality-bibbers. The play was a well-crafted nothing which would ensure it a long run, even after the television series had ended. At the interval, Edward did not leave his seat. This was because he needed to concentrate on resolving a very important question. He was no stage-door Johnny. That was impossibly vulgar. Felicity was an actress of distinction who would no doubt treat such approaches with irreproachable charm but inner contempt. But he could not simply behave as though he were someone scuttling back to a coach bound for Dartford. He wanted to make some demonstration of his appreciation of her art. He did not want to let the occasion go. He did not dare to pronounce the word that was in his heart, preferring to take refuge in the neutral term 'admiration'.

As the bell rang and the audience began to file back to its seats (was that man's horrible scraping of his ice-cream carton going to finish before the second act began?) Edward was still unsure of his strategy. Felicity's performance in the second half settled the question for him. Her verbal fencing with the loathsome husband was exquisite and the sudden race of her doomed but thrilling passion for her reluctant lover silenced even the chattering pensioners from Penge. It was heartbreaking, though the humour saved it from any mawkishness. At the final curtain the audience was ecstatic and Edward lost himself in the collective enthusiasm. After the very last curtain-call, he carefully felt under his seat to retrieve a small paper package which he shielded from the crush of exiting playgoers.

Outside, in the glitter of neon and approaching head-lights, a small crowd gathered around the stage door. Edward felt uncomfortable to be at the edge of this cluster and pretended to walk away. Then he returned and went away again. He was nervous and uncertain. And then she emerged, accepting gratefully a small bouquet, scribbling her autograph on several programmes, smiling with benign tolerance as she moved firmly towards a waiting cab. She was just about to drive off when Edward approached the open window of the cab through which she was handing a last autograph. Hoping that his dignified manner would distinguish him from the autograph-hunters (an unspeakable pastime) he leaned towards her and said: 'I found your performance, Miss Cazamian, quite exceptional.' As she smiled at him in the only way possible, with queenly grace, he produced apparently from nowhere a single blue rose (red would have been cheap and vulgar) which a gloved hand seized near the top of the stem.

As the train rattled back to the northern suburbs her gracious words: 'How beautiful, how kind of you!' reverberated in his mind. Edward patted the programme on his knee and thought of how the gifted wrought a change on the world and how love could take many forms, and how without it we were nothing more than that inert wooden seat which stood there, at this station-pause, empty and isolated under a pool of light.

# 22. OF MISUNDERSTANDINGS

IF LOVERS KNEW how to behave. If they kept their cool. If they used a bit of common... But of course that isn't to be. They are always making mistakes and letting their passions run away with them. If they didn't – yes, yes, I know – it wouldn't be love.

Pyramus and Thisbe were in love. He was the boy next door and she was the girl. Building regulations in Thebes were not what they are now and a chink had opened up in the cavity wall between the Pyramus and Thisbe residences. By this means the lovers could communicate but, without going into the vulgarity of particulars, this wasn't quite enough. The fierce disapproval of their parents (tell me about it, groan the young lovers of the world to this day) kept the two apart until they could bear it no more.

They arranged to meet secretly in a graveyard (the proximity of the dead at one of those scenes where we are most alive a nice touch from the poets). Thisbe arrived first, draped in a white shawl to preserve her *incognito*. Looking up and down the gloomy rows of headstones she could see no sign of her lover. 'Love made her bold,' Ovid observes at this point, but very soon she saw something else that took her boldness away. An angry lioness prowling the night also caught sight of Thisbe and advanced menacingly. So quickly did she make her escape that her white veil fell to the ground and there was really no possibility of stooping to retrieve it. The lioness padded up to the spot and sniffed and picked at the fallen veil with her blood-soaked jaws (having just eaten) in order to ascertain that there was nothing worth making a meal of underneath it. Then she lumbered off for a post-prandial snooze.

At this point Pyramus – who had got into the usual where-do-you-think-you're-going-at-this-time-of-night riff with his folks – arrived late by the moonlit tomb only to discover that Thisbe was nowhere to be seen. He took a few turns around the graveyard before his eye fell on the bloody veil. Letting out a howl of grief he jumped – as lovers always do – to the wrong conclusion and lamented his lost love, whom he had enjoyed merely through a chink in the wall. Cursing the lion who had consumed his beloved and seeing no point in going on living (another tendency of young lovers but one that generally remains at the level of sobbing rhetoric) he took out his sword and fell forward on its point. Moments later, Thisbe arrived and her laments were even louder than her unfortunate lover's. Howling and shrieking into the clammy night air she picked up the sword that had been used by Pyramus and repeated his action so that, because of a failure to check the facts, the lives of two young lovers were rubbed out. This pointless immolation is remembered – if you believe the poet Ovid – in the purple hue of the mulberry tree which was white as the moonlight that night but ever since, drenched in the spurting blood of Pyramus, has shown a different colour.

Felix arrived at the island on the overnight ferry. They walked up to the little village three kilometres from the port where a taverna was open. They chose one of the tables scattered outside and shaded from the hot sun by the branches of a mulberry tree. A plate of fried fish, a carafe of wine, were brought out to them under the tree on the stones which were stained by the fallen fruit, squashed underfoot to release an ooze of juice like a dark seep of blood.

Afterwards they slept the long sleep of the exhausted who have been taken in and well fed on a sunny afternoon under the branches of a mulberry tree.

## 23. IT NEVER ENDS

HERE IS AN affecting tale of an eighty-year-old man who has found love. Literature mocks the lustiness, the out of sequence amours of the aged. Saucy old bugger, they say, elbowing each other in the ribs. Ought to be past it at his age. Love, it seems, becomes undignified with age. What was splendid at twenty is an embarrassment at eighty. Could it be that we have got this wrong?

Old men take many forms. They can be angry and belliger-ent, crusty and difficult, bitter and tyrannical. They can be, not to mince words, old gits. But they can also be – and isn't this how we all want to end up? – mellow and ripe. After a life-time of raging at the world (which is something one has little choice but to do) there's something to be said for hanging up one's boots, filling a pipe, and striking the pose of the ripened sage, the man who's seen it all and won't see some of it again. Just before one departs, a little wisdom, a little ripeness, a hand run through the bin of yellow grain, a knowing knead-ing between finger and thumb, the delivery of a verdict.

And of course, these precious characteristics are to be applied to women, too.

At the end of a life one can either regret the performance or turn it over gratefully in one's mind. With health and strength and a full belly and a seat in the sun it might be possible to say: things aren't so bad. Things could be worse. If the man or woman is a thinker there might even have been the attainment of some wisdom – though that's a tricky concept, for sometimes we need to be foolish. Wisdom can involve playing safe. But there is a need – at some stage in a life – to play with fire.

It is the man's eightieth birthday and he has surprised and not surprised everyone by announcing that it is also to be his wedding day. His children, holding a lunch in his honour elsewhere, are informed. Moments later, they emerge from their private dining-room singing a traditional wedding song. For this is not the coldly formal world of wet roofs and grey skies and suburban lawns. It is Africa. The bridegroom (whose wife is twenty seven years younger) is a man of great calm and dignity. He is not an old git. Because he is the President of his country the newspapers are full of nuptial excitement. His old enemies – who put him in jail, who threatened him with the gallows, who made him live in a solitary cell, who made him slop out toilet-buckets and hack at stones in the hot sun, are now as excited as anyone. They send him their congratulations. Have they remembered that twenty seven years is the period they kept him on the prison island? His new wife has given them a useful mnemonic.

The President is a forgiving man. So forgiving and so dignified and so apparently without hate that we call him a saint. Which may be true for saints are always flawed, their goodness offset by the jagged frame of ordinary humanity. His friend from the prison island tells the newspapers that he was a man of great strength and determination and courage and resolve. Playing chess with a cellmate he told the warders to lock away the board at the end of the day. He repeated the instruction at the end of the second day but halfway through the third, his opponent conceded defeat. He could not go on playing chess with this man of iron, this man who could see from afar what he wanted and who proceeded, not in rushed steps, not breathless, to obtain it. Perhaps saints are difficult to live with. Perhaps the best thing is to step aside and let them get on with it.

The cruel authorities sometimes pretended to be kind. They offered their now famous prisoner better conditions. They said he need not collect the buckets nor go out to the quarry with his pick and shovel. But he refused, saying that all were equal in that place. That is the sort of thing that saints say. They are also human. The old man, in his younger days, was a little vain. He refused to shave off his beard to make himself more invisible to the police and the sentries at roadblocks because he was attached to his magnificent fungus. Pictures of him appeared on the walls of student digs and inner city squats and the beard was always there as it was always there in the pictures of Che Guevara. But Che was a Latin with a black beret and his beard was straggly and romantic.

So let us leave the old man on his birthday/wedding day, walking in the hot African sun, smiling among the crowds, thinking to himself, perhaps, that the air is good and that it is not such a bad idea, all things considered, to be alive.

# 24. THE FOREST OF MORROIZ

AFTER MANY VICISSITUDES (a reference to battles with giants, random invitations to joust, arrows tipped with poison, encounters with unidentified knights in black, maidens locked in stone towers, periods of recuperation from wounds in desolate abbeys, complaining knights at fountains in the depths of lonely forests, turbulent sea journeys, mistaken identities, bouts of madness, lamentations) Tristan – whom King Mark of Cornwall loathed more than anyone on earth because of his obsession with his wife Iseut – was captured one day in bed with the Queen. Unarmed (in the nature of the case) he was carried off by a platoon of beefy churls to a place of execution. Their path lay along the Cornish coast where Tristan saw his opportunity at a lonely church on the cliff top with rocks and seething surf below. With death staring him in the face he experienced a surge of extra energy, snapped his ropes, laid out at least one churl immediately by grabbing the latter's sword, and leapt over the cliff.

Later, this became known as Tristan's Leap.

But Tristan, of course, was not dead, simply lodged on a shelf of rock where he was found by his friend Fergus. Meanwhile the Queen, who in one version of the story had been condemned to the unpleasant fate of being tossed to the mercies of a gang of lusty lepers, and in another had merely been rescued from the palace at Tintagel by Tristan's loyal companion Gorvenal, was brought to the blustery coastline. The two lovers were thus re-united, pondering their next move. It was Tristan who came up with the idea of an arboreal love nest.

At the heart of the Forest of Morroiz, near a rock called

the Wise Damsel's Rock (I know), there was a beautiful house surrounded by trickling fountains and lush gardens and fruitful orchards. Tristan proposed that this rustic hideaway should be their home from now on, their bosky utopia. He did not understand, being neither an etymologist nor a classical scholar, that utopia is nowhere to be found, that human beings claim to yearn for a Paradise that in reality will start to give them itchy feet on Day One. Iseut, being a woman, was infinitely more shrewd.

'Tristan,' she said. 'If we lived for ever in this place the world would recede. We would lose it and it would lose us. We would be cut off from the mainstream of life. There would be no tournaments, and knightly *chic*. No palace intrigues, no courtly *couture*, no social life, no stimulus, no news, no gossip, no life.'

But try telling that to a man who has been bound by churls, who has just escaped from certain death and who has leaped over a cliff to save his skin. The illusion of the inviolable love-nest runs strong in such male brains and can't be prised out with something as humdrum as a little bit of old-fashioned common sense. So he gave her the old line about it just being the two of us and we were the whole world and nothing else mattered. At the end of his spiel, Iseut realised that she had little choice but to mask her misgivings and say yes. And so he took her to the rock of the Wise Damsel, showing her the house (like a cunning estate agent) in its best light, promising her fresh spring-water and daily joints of venison. And with the clever practical touch of one pointing out that a Safeway is only ten miles drive away from the village, he observed that any specialist supplies could be had from a nearby castle. And so the two lovers lived in Paradise.

But because it was Paradise it could not last.

Every day Tristan hunted. He hunted and hunted until they were sick of fresh venison. On one hunting expedition he left Iseut at home, playing chess with her maid. As chance would have it, the King of Cornwall, straying from his main hunting party, ended up in the vicinity. He asked a few shepherds whom he found resting by a spring if they had seen Tristan and they jerked their thumbs in the right direction. A little later King Mark returned with a mob of knights, armed to the teeth, and plucked Iseut away from her chess-game, away from her rustic idyll. They pulled the plug on Paradise. Iseut was locked up in a stone tower to prevent any further misdemeanours and instructions were issued for everyone to hunt down Tristan whose guts were required for the King's garters. What happened next was that a youth with a quiver of poisoned arrows, spotting Tristan in the Forest, discharged one of his arrows at the knight. Tristan limped off, his body immediately having swelled up with the poison. There was only one person who had the skills in herbal medicine to cure Tristan: Iseut of the White Hands was the last hope.

Tristan and the trusty Gorvenal took ship to Brittany where the daughter of the King of that country would use her knowledge of alternative medicine to heal the swollen knight. And, as I think you can guess, there were further consequences of this encounter with the fair Iseut.

Perhaps Tristan, as he lay in the bottom of the Brittany ferry, writhing in pain and thinking that his days were numbered, reflected that utopia was truly the place that is not. He would realise that love cannot feed off itself but needs to work itself out in the world – which has an odd way of letting us know that we can't escape it. Iseut was right in her initial misgivings when she was shown the estate agent's particulars. She knew that a perfect view and the sound of gurgling fountains and chirping birdsong would begin, in the end, to pall.

But try telling that to the countless lovers who, as we speak, are combing the lists for their own secluded love-nest deep in the heart of their earmarked Forest of Morroiz.

# 25. THE LOVE OF JUSTICE

THE SMALLER OF the two men leaned across to the brass disk by the door which had at its centre, white and veined like the ball of an eye, a smooth porcelain push which read: PRESS. They could faintly hear the bell echo deep inside the dark lobby of the old Victorian house on the seafront with its three green gables looking out on the estuary where perhaps an oil-tanker or a tiny coaster throbbed slowly out into the Irish Sea. The little man, Joe Ashcroft, stepped back and waited. His companion was burly and red-faced. He had the sort of preening pomposity that could have earned him a casting in a cinematic Dickens adaptation. He wore a heavy overcoat and a scarf was tightly bound around his neck. When the door opened he lifted off his tweed trilby to greet the person whom he would almost certainly have described as the lady of the house.

The contrasting pair were led inside to the drawing-room and offered coffee. Mr Adams cast a quick, experienced eye around the room. He saw less than he had hoped. His container at the docks was only half full and he had three weeks left before he returned to Canada. He oughtn't really to be sitting around drinking coffee. Making small-talk, he asked the boy what he was going to do with his life.

'I'd like to be a journalist, Mr Adams.'

'In my country,' Mr Adams replied, puffing out his chest into a dignified rebuttal of indecorous thoughts and unwise proposals, 'a journalist is a drunken bum.'

Felix's parents looked at each other quickly and changed the subject to the question of antiques. Mr Adams was brutally frank. The only piece he wanted was the one that they would not part with and his mission, thanks to the over-eager promotion of Joe Ashcroft, was a futile one. Only three weekends to go and half a container to fill. But Joe showed no signs of hurry, the half-witted little creature.

Joe stepped out into the garden where everyone had carried their coffee-cups. His scarred, stubby fingers felt the stitching of a hammock strung up between two posts. He examined closely the material and rubbed the fabric between his finger and thumb. He pulled at the rope. He could have made a better job for half the price but no-one cared any more about craftsmanship. They preferred cheap imports sold at the big stores. He walked down to the bottom of the garden, followed by Felix who had decided that he was the more interesting of the two men. He looked out into the distance at the grey stretch of water at low tide, the red buoys, and a single boat visible on the water. The port was in decline. The big liners had gone. Not many worked on the docks now. He started to tell Felix the story of how they had mustered every morning at the dock gates for work. In a large open space inside the gates they had gathered to be hired. Some of the men leaped on the backs of the men in front, signalling frantically to the foreman their desperation for work. Joe had shouted at them: "Get down, men. Get down. Where's your dignity?'

He turned away from the sea and looked directly at the boy.

'I'm as humble as a beggar, but I've got my dignity.'

# 26. ANOTHER JOKE

UNCLE DERMOT TOLD one of his jokes about a docker who suddenly started to run when he reached the dock gates after a shift. The dock-gate policeman ran after him, the two men's legs pounding up and down, faces puffed and breathing heavily. The docker had got as far as The Caradoc when he felt the policeman's hand on his collar.

'Right, John, empty your pockets.'

'It's alright, officer, I've got nothing on me.'

Uncle Dermot grinned comfortably while his audience waited patiently for the punchline.

'I was just practising for tomorrow night.'

# 27. CARPE DIEM

IF THERE ARE lessons of love we are all poor pupils. We go on making the same mistakes. But here's a sure and fast rule, an axiom, a chip off the logarithmic table, a racing certainty, a law. Love doesn't stand still so grab it while you can.

Horace, Book One, Number Eleven.

'Come in number eleven, your time is up.'

Don't try and forecast the future or hedge your bets, Horace says. You can't know what tomorrow will bring so make the most of this moment. Live for today. *Carpe diem, quam minimum credula postero.* Seize the day, put as little faith as you can in what *might* come. Enjoy what *has* come. The problem with simple truths, however, is that we ignore them. We think the answer ought to be more clever and so we take our eye off the ball.

And someone else scores.

The poets have always liked this line of argument.

'I bet they have. Boys to a man.'

'Yes, but, Trish.'

'Don't yesbut me. They like the idea of 'seizing their pleasure' from any dame who happens to be in their field of vision – especially when we aren't talking consequences here.'

'Take Andrew Marvell's *To his Coy Mistress.*'

'That's just what we have to do. Take it. Look at that title for example.'

'Well, if we're on the subject of looking, I suggest you look at it a little more closely. OK, the mistress isn't identified but then we don't know much about her lover either unless you think it's autobiographical.'

'From what I've heard that's unlikely. Andy wasn't exactly a lady's man if you catch my drift.'

My point is that it's an argument, an intelligent argument between equals. He sets out his stall. He puts his cards on the table. He says that ideally this shouldn't be done in a hurry and that she deserves more time than anyone could humanly give and more. But the snag is that the clock is ticking. And it's ticking for both of them. There's no pleasure if they wait until the undertakers drive up in their long black cars and thick overcoats, their pale faces putting on a solemn look that means nothing. Poetry will be no use by then: sex, beauty, lust, passion, mutual pleasure all lobbed into a skip. So the obvious thing is to take it while it's on offer. For *both* of them to take it while it's on offer. To live, briefly, at a higher rate (and isn't that the definition of love?), to poke Time in the eye, is the deal he's offering and what woman or man would refuse? This is an adult argument for adult lovers. It's for people who have lived and want to live some more before the park-keeper comes, jangling his keys and whistling in the suburban twilight. The argument is as cool as a cucumber but the feeling behind it could melt a planet.

> *Thus, though we cannot make our Sun*
> *Stand still, yet we will make him run.*

That's the note, Trish, the true note of love. Hubris. The extra mile. The walk on the wild side. Putting everything into the wager, letting go, throwing caution to the winds. Choose your own cliché from our tempting selection.

And it's exactly the same for her. This is the most equal love poem I know: the first person plural is its grammar.

# 28. THE LOVE OF CHILDREN

'WHOOPS!'

'There's a word for this.'

**WRITER'S LOONY LOVE-BOOK PLUGS PAEDOPHILIA**

'Relax, Trish, I'm only winding you up.'

I was thinking, again, of Lewis Carroll, of the man we're too busy wrapping up in interpretations to understand. We paste labels on him until he looks like an old-fashioned cabin trunk, but we don't know where he's going. He took pictures of little girls so we know he was a dirty old man. Poor, sad, upper-class Englishman with whiskers and an uncomfortable collar, and cold Oxford rooms with port and frozen windows and toast browning on the tip of a brass fork. And only bottled-up love to boost the heat and terrible, drippy, droopy, damp, melancholy, bitter-sweet English sadness in his heart. Turn up that Elgar. Where's that perishing lark?

Shouldn't these boys get out in the sun a bit more?

But what if he took those photographs of the little girls not because he was a thief, a snatcher of innocence, a despoiler, but because he saw them not as pretty little girls but as young women who would go places? Here we are in the gallery, peering at the tiny prints. Here is a not-so-pretty young woman who will be a pioneer of women's education. I can hear the SPLAT! of a rubber stamp crashing down on the print and it reads FORMIDABLE. This lady is going places the way a steamroller goes places. Get out of the way, wimps and people-who-can-think-of-reasons-why-not.

But coming back to the girls in Chinese costume posed prettily on a tasteful tumble of lacquered boxes. Look again.

Look a little more closely. These are not 'objects'. These are subjects, these are real people, with complicated expressions and uncrumpling intelligence and unfurling thoughts. The photographer is giving them something. What is it? Let's look again. He's giving them themselves, their individuality. They are looking at him as if they were looking through him and beyond him, through the looking-glass into a world of wonder, a world of excitement and growth through which their beauty and intelligence might find a way, might do great things. Perhaps we have got it wrong. Perhaps the world of Victorian childhood which we pity was...

'For the rich little girls...'

...a world of imaginative freedom and time and books and long walks and hoops and games that a frantically busy work-work world has lost.

Now I *am* getting sentimental.

'I'm saying nothing. Or rather, I'm not so sure about your dodgy Dodgson thesis. Haven't you heard the news?'

'No, but you're going to tell me.'

'The international police have just cracked a particularly nasty paedophile ring on the Internet. Trading in images of young boys and girls. Really horrible stuff. And do you know what this group of perverts called itself?'

'Again, you are going to tell me.'

'The Wonderland Club.'

*'O Oysters, come and walk with us!'*
*The Walrus did beseech.*
*'A pleasant walk, a pleasant talk,*
*Along the briny beach.'*

Can love ever be equal? Doesn't love – of things as much as of people – always get itself mixed up with wanting to have as well as to hold? I want to possess her. I can't have her. You are mine. I am yours.

# 29. THE LOVE OF COUNTRY

THE WELSH HAVE a word for it. *Hwyl.*

It means the bond that men and women have with their native soil.

That's always struck me as an odd expression. I was born from a living womb not a handful of dirt. I think of myself as a pilgrim not an anchorite. It's true that we all come from somewhere or other. We come from there but we have moved on. We might circle back. We might have fond memories. We might have nightmares of recollection, but the native heath is only a starting-point, a launch-pad. The most passionate patriots are the ones who don't live in their own patch. They are singing songs of home in the smoky bars of exile, elaborating their pain. But why don't they come home?

The Welshman, Saunders Lewis, the patriot with the ever-so-slightly-dodgy politics, once declared: *Civilization must be more than an abstraction. It must have a local habitation and a name. Here, its name is Wales.*

Isn't that fair enough? One is always complaining about the homogenisation of the world, of the great steam iron of global capitalism, flattening out all the ripples and rucks and creases. These people with their songs and their embroidered caps and their funny phrases and their treasured pictures above the fish-fryer, are helping to keep the world interesting for wanderers and pilgrims and pokers about in the world's spaces like oneself. That swinging Madonna suspended from the bus-driver's rear view mirror means more to you than you think. Don't knock it, mate.

Fair enough, but what about the dark side, the downside? Love of my patch becomes hatred of your patch or – which

76

is rather more to the point – hatred of anyone who strays onto my patch. The dispossessed build their huts by the river but they don't seem to be too bothered about the people who also want to fish and rub their clothes on the stones and plant their rows of beans but who wear their hats in a different way. Love of one's soil isn't worth much if it becomes hatred of the other guy's soil. (You can see how I am trying to avoid mentioning the word Bosnia.)

So what am I saying? That I take the point about the drunkenness of things being various but that if you are going to ask me to be patriotic you must find me a way of doing so that is open not closed, that involves welcoming the stranger with a leaf of basil and a tot of rough, red wine and a piece of that delicious pie that's just come back from the baker's oven.

It is December. It is late afternoon in the high sheep-country of central Wales and the light is failing. Then it starts to snow. The flakes drift across the open moorland, across the unfenced and unhedged road. Two shapes appear, not yet eclipsed by the hurrying dark. They are wearing long, dirty green macs and their belts are made of rope. They are driving a small flock of ragged sheep before them. When the car passes, they do not turn towards the headlamps. They trudge on, snowflakes melting on their stubbled chins, their eyes set straight ahead, walking into the dark, walking into the mountain and their solitude, wordless and intent.

From the ninth century Welsh of Llywarch Hen:

*I am old, I am lonely, I am shapeless and cold after my honoured couch; I am wretched, I am bent in three.*

*I am bent in three and old, I am peevish and giddy, I am silly, I am cantankerous; those who loved me love me not.*

## 30. QUACK, QUACK

DR FREUD OBSERVED (a man who, at the start of a new century, wobbles uncertainly on his marble pedestal) that: 'In one class of cases being in love is no more than object-cathexis on the part of the sexual instincts with a view to directly sexual satisfaction, a cathexis which expires, more-over, when this aim has been reached; this is what is called common, sensual love.'

One is tempted to shout, from the back of the class: 'You're not wrong, Doc!' Except for a nagging doubt about the meaning of these terms. Cathexis. Dimly, we think we catch his drift. He would seem to have worked out what it all boils down to.

But has he? Even the Viennese Quack himself had to concede 'a whole scale of possibilities within the range of the phenomena of love'. Adjusting those round-rimmed spectacles and rubbing forefinger and thumb through his wiry white beard, the Doctor considered how: 'In connec-tion with the question of being in love we have always been struck by the phenomenon of sexual overvaluation, the fact that the loved object enjoys a certain amount of freedom from criticism, and that all its characteristics are valued more highly than those of people who are not loved, or than its own were at a time when it itself was not loved.'

With the great gravity of the honoured sage he pronounced his truth. I should have liked to have been there, in that gloomy study in old Vienna when the Doctor shuffled his notes and shouted: 'Eureka!'

'...The tendency which falsifies judgement in this respect is that of *idealization*.'

Yes, the great man has got it in one. Well done, old Sigmund: when we're smitten, it's goodbye to common sense.

In the same way, Tristan, taking the magic potion – which is a rather nicer way of putting it than object-cathexis-what-ever-that-might-mean – no longer saw the daughter of the King of Ireland, whom he was ferrying home with the professional detachment of a late-night cabbie, but someone else: The Object of His Love. And his ego and his id and his overflowing narcissistic libido, and a great deal else besides, were thrown up into the air and when they clattered down on the wooden deck of the boat he was all at sea. Certain commentators have ingeniously suggested that the adulter-ous love of Tristan and Iseut, which on the face of it was not *exactly* the thing that mediaeval Christendom preferred to have celebrated by every *jongleur* in town, was made accept-able by the magic potion. A good Catholic would have gone into the confessional, collected his *Hail Marys*, and tried – for at least the rest of the day – to snap out of it. But if he had been handed a silver goblet brimming with magic potion there would have been no point. He could have no moral responsibility for what happened, no brake of conscience, no bless-me-father-for-I-have-sinned. It was all down to the magic, you see.

At the back of the classroom, Felix opened the blue Catechism and turned to the back pages which were not the ones which they were required to learn. Everyone knew the easy ones off by heart:

– *Why did God make you?*

– *God made me to know him, love him and serve him in this world, and to be happy with him for ever in the next.*

But there were other questions and other answers.

– *What does the sixth Commandment forbid?*

– *The sixth Commandment forbids all sins of impurity with another's wife and husband.*

When Tristan entered the chamber of Iseut, where flames danced in the enormous hearth and the oak tables and dressers reeked of beeswax polish; when he drew back the embroidered coverlet to gaze on the nakedness of another's wife, he was well out of order in sixth Commandment terms, but the alternative, folks, doesn't sell books.

*The sixth Commandment forbids immodest songs, books and pictures, because they are most dangerous to the soul and lead to mortal sin.*

And if you didn't get the point with number six, try number nine, the one about coveting thy neighbour's wife: *the ninth Commandment forbids all wilful consent to impure thoughts and desires, and all wilful pleasure in the irregular motions of the flesh.*

Felix knelt in the side pews at the back of the Church waiting for the confessional to become free. He searched his conscience for some useful minor sins to act as padding or bubblewrap for the terrible Big One that blackened his heart. His strategy would be to sidle up to it slowly, fencing behind the I-have-told-lies and the I-have-been-disobedients, waiting for the moment to strike home quickly. His flesh was tortured with irregular motions. Impure thoughts and desires fired his imagination. He knew that these things were a matter of using the right language, finding the code that would be understood by the solitary man behind the black curtain that hung across the tiny grille. He settled for 'being impure', and the priest played the game, sending him out with his freight of penitential prayers. Felix, briefly, felt clean again. Not pure exactly, but a little less impure. Later, much later, he would learn that impurity is like the air we breathe and it is the pure who should frighten us with their cleaning-up exercises, their stiff broom sweeping up all the people-who-are-not-like-us into a giant dustpan and sliding the contents into the dustbin of history.

As he repeated the silent prayers he looked towards the

still altar with its plaster saints whose outstretched palms or naked flanks showed painted wounds. Rows of spluttering candles flamed on a curved black metal rack. A small scatter of pious parishioners knelt, their heads down, apart in their worlds of contemplation, communing with something. Perhaps they, too, had irregular motions of the flesh. Perhaps they too were wilful. Impure.

– What is perfect contrition?

– *Perfect contrition is sorrow for sin arising purely from the love of God.*

# 31. THE GREEN-EYED MONSTER

THE LOVE OF Tristan and Iseut was at once like no other and like every other love. Which is perhaps another way of saying that its course was more like a bumpy ride in a cart whose wheels were hooped in iron than it was a soft purr over the tarmac in the supple leather of some industrial magnate's Roller.

Felix remembered the long file of football supporters shuffling along a cobbled street in the direction of the turn-stiles. They stopped, parting like a biblical sea, when a white Rolls Royce appeared. The rich man inside, whose riches came from their blue and pink football-pool vouchers on which tiny crosses were drawn in blue Biro, smiled like a gratified monarch as they let him through on his way to the directors' car park and the cold drinks behind glass, and the smiles and solidarity of old, hairless men with invisible cummerbunds of banknotes wrapped around their fat bellies.

When Tristan arrived in Brittany, to be cured by the deli-cate white hands and herbal know-how of the beautiful Iseut in her green embroidered gown of silk, he looked on the daughter of King Hoel and began to feel, what he ought not to have felt, the stirrings of something like the love he felt for the other Iseut, blaming the whole thing on the accidental matching of their names. Tristan, like the small boy in the confessional, began to Examine His Conscience. He saw that his love for Iseut of Cornwall was wrong. Perhaps, therefore, it was right to love Iseut of Brittany, whose deli-cate white hands mixed him a herbal cocktail that would end his pain, draining away the horrible pus and allowing his skin to grow whole again. And so he married version two of Iseut. But on his wedding night he remembered version one and the love they had known ever since they quaffed the magic philtre at sea and fell under the sway of love's absolute tyranny. So intense was his remembering of the first Iseut that he could not bring himself to do what men and women are supposed to do on their wedding-night. Instead he merely held Iseut of the White Hands in his arms. Being an innocent young Breton princess she imagined that there was no more to sharing a bed than this and was perfectly happy. With his arms around her, Tristan felt a pain that no herbal remedies could extinguish and longed in his heart for the first Iseut, locked in her Cornish tower by the angry King Mark.

After a year of this torment, Tristan was out riding on the sea shore with Iseut's brother Kahedin when he confessed his dilemma. With no thought to family solidarity, Kahedin immediately sympathised with his brother-in-law's predicament and suggested that there was nothing for it but to ditch his sister and return to Cornwall. This was exactly what Tristan wanted to hear and he resolved to take Kahedin with him, the latter having expressed a desire for a glimpse of this nonpareil. When Iseut of Cornwall's faithful servant Brangain turned up with a sorrowful letter from her mistress pleading with Tristan to return to his first and truest love, that was the end of any havering or should-we-or-shouldn't-we. Tristan and Kahedin went straight to the docks, and after various vicissitudes (which included, naturally enough an encounter with the Knight of the Howling Beast), they arrived back in Cornwall where Tristan was secretly re-united with the one and only Iseut. All night they did the things from which Tristan restrained himself on his wedding night with Iseut of the White Hands.

But at this point the iron wheels of the cart of love suddenly struck an obstinate rock in the middle of the track which sent the occupants flying. Kahedin, the loyal knight who had been so sympathetic to Tristan's need to cast his sister to the wind, finally set eyes on Iseut and was instantly smitten. He was thrown into agonies of grief and despair because he knew he could not have Iseut of Cornwall and he cursed the day he ever agreed, as they galloped along the wet sands of the Brittany coast, to accompany Tristan on his voyage to Cornwall. After writhing in pain and cursing his fate and generally torturing himself in the way prescribed for unfortunate lovers, Kahedin suddenly jumped out of bed and called for some parchment and ink. He sat at an oak table in his apartment and scribbled a furious, desperate letter to Iseut. He told her that he was in love, that he could do nothing about it, that it was tearing him in pieces and that he would soon be dead if things went on the way they had been going. When she received the letter, Iseut was astonished. Eight centuries later we might have said she was gobsmacked.

She read the letter again, this time with the cogs of her brain engaged. She decided that Tristan would not be too pleased if she allowed his friend to die of grief so she called for her writing materials and drafted a clever reply. She made it seem as if she sympathised. She dropped a few hints and let a little light shine into the darkness of Kahedin's soul. In this way, she thought, he would recover and when he was once again *compos mentis* he could be told to pull himself together, to stop being so daft and to catch the boat back to Brittany.

One doesn't have to be totally immersed in mediaeval love-literature – those little pink books by the supermarket checkout contain much the same sort of material – to know that letters between lovers and letters between third parties and the criss-crossings of this mail, errors in sorting and delivery and the correct setting-out of the address, cause all sorts of ructions in the average love-life. On them plots turn every bit as much as mistaken identities, disguises, or chance encounters in the moonlight. And so it was, that entering Kahedin's apartment – for the two friends were always in and out of each other's lodgings – Tristan happened to notice a well-thumbed letter in a familiar hand, lying on the bed. Snatching it up, and reading Iseut's consoling words to the love-lorn knight, he went ballistic. All Iseut's sly nuances and duplicitous come-ons and tantalising hints were lost on the raging knight. At the next available opportunity he accosted Kahedin in the Queen's turret and threatened him with instant death. Not entirely sure of the sequence of events and unaware that his treasured letter had been read by Tristan, Kahedin nonetheless saw what was in Tristan's mind and dived immediately through the window, landing on the soft green lawn where King Mark and Queen Iseut were having a quiet game of open-air chess, surrounded by a thicket of Cornish knights who were commenting on the game and muttering their opinions on the quality of the moves. Any one of them would have rushed at Tristan with a chopper had they known he was secretly in the Queen's apartments so all the knight could do was to fume silently by the arras. With great presence of mind (and already having guessed the truth) the Queen jumped up and said that Kahedin must have fallen asleep by the window then keeled over. The courtiers seemed to buy this argument and the chess-game resumed. It wasn't until later that Tristan and the Queen were able to have words. Tristan was so mad that he had put on his armour, and was spoiling for a fight...

'A typical *macho* response. Blame the woman, threaten violence, wave your chopper about. This all has a familiar ring.'

'Yes, but Trish...'

'There you go again yesbutting and excusing. Just get on with the story.'

Tristan, so heavily swathed in macho-metal that no-one

could recognise him, wouldn't let the Queen explain and stormed out of the castle, walking past the courtiers who, if they had been able to see under his helmet, would have hurled every available lance in the castle at him. With his metal clanking and rattling, and with some very nasty curses on his breath, Tristan stomped through Tintagel, getting madder and madder by the minute. In this mood it wasn't long before he picked a fight with a wandering knight called Giglain who got in his way. This little encounter was witnessed by King Mark who happened to be loafing in one of the turrets. He sent his men down to interrogate poor Giglain who had come off worst in the engagement. From his account he realised that his opponent must have been Tristan. When Giglain revealed that Tristan was so mad with Iseut that he had packed his bags and made himself scarce, the King was overjoyed. At last his rival was out of his hair.

Meanwhile Tristan left Tintagel behind and plunged deeper into the dark forest and deeper into the darkness of despair. Not to put too fine a point on it, he went mad. Nor should it surprise anyone to learn that the Queen was in a similar state. And all because of a misunderstanding about a letter which no-one would sit still enough and listen long enough to see was not what it appeared to be. But since when did lovers behave rationally and calmly, taking in all angles, and seeing everything whole? And when the green-eyed monster of jealousy, the slippery snake of mistrust, slithers into the room no-one can avoid being bitten. With their typical logic lovers argue that this is simply the flip-side of love. If you didn't care so strongly for your lover you wouldn't go so mad so quickly and so absolutely. Not to get het-up is to be indifferent and what has indifference got to do with love?

# 32. OF MICE AND MEN

WHEN THE RAINS of autumn come the mice drift in from the fields, plump and well-fed at this time of year, their coats honey-coloured, their shirt fronts smooth and white, for these are the kempt country-mice, not the dirty town guttersnipes who snuffle and scurry in the black dust between the railway lines in Charing Cross Underground station. But they have the same bad habits of incontinence that make them as unwelcome in the country cottages as in the steamy restaurant kitchens where public health inspectors go. And the same appetite for cheese. The humans, who never seem quite cunning enough, place cubes of cheese on the spike of a mousetrap (they should think of using nuts which can be recycled for future deaths – a free piece of advice) and wait to see, at day break, if they have caught their prey. But the mouse is a dainty eater, whose fine teeth can sometimes make short work of a cube of cheese without springing the fatal CLACK! of the metal jaws of the trap. Yet he does not always escape and the owner of the cottage – who always feels a little sad at this, on successful mornings lifts up the trap and inspects the rigid corpse, the flattened nose, the teeth still clamped on the tiny hazel nut like a freeze-frame camera shot, the eyes bright and beady. He takes it outside and shakes it free from the trap into a shallow pit that has been dug with a trowel. He quickly covers the little corpse with soil, disguising the work of death.

On a hot August day, Felix rode with the other members of the gang in the back of the open truck, out through the tangle of factories and dual carriageways and roundabouts and patches of derelict land that are the untidy backyard of the city's scruffy, petering-out conurbation. They passed through what might once have been considered the countryside, past old red-brick inns with country-sounding names. They brushed hedges blackened with road-dirt and dust, they passed fields in which horses stood disconsolately in groups. Then more roads and factories and housing estates and big roadhouses with full carparks. Then Ron, the Scotsman, said: 'This is it.' They exchanged some banter with the man on the gate then bumped through in the truck to the edge of the enormous power station. Ron grinned:

'This is the drill, Felix, you fucking intellectual. That there is a heap of chippings. That is a barrow. And that is a spade. All you have to do is spend the rest of the day moving that lot to the far end of this gap until there's no pile left. The good news is that by the time you've finished you'll be at this end. Any questions?'

Felix looked at the long path of flattened clay that ran down the side of the power station wall. It seemed very long and the pile of stones dumped on the ground by a lorry first thing that morning seemed rather high. It was eight thirty and the sun was already burning in the clear blue sky. He joined the other three at the tailgate of the truck, pulling out the spades and barrows. Ron was grinning as usual as he dashed forward to fill the first barrow.

'So you're studying poetry and that? I know lots of poetry. I'm nae a fuckin' ignorant Scotsman, you know what I mean? I had an old-fashioned Scottish education. Keats. Wordsworth. I know it all.'

Ron pulled the barrow back from the pile, twisted it round, and began to heave forward.

*The king sits in Dunfermline town*
*Drinking the blude-red wine;*
*O whare will I get a skeely skipper*
*To sail this new ship o' mine*

D'ye know who wrote that, Felix you fucker? It was Anon.

He was a great poet. But we don't know who the fucker was. He could have been any of us or all of us. He could have been a fucker like me. Aye, that's me. Anon.'

Ron was out of earshot now and the other three men fell to work, sweating steadily, shovelling and heaving their loaded barrows down the path. As he worked, and as the heat rose, Felix became aware of a foul smell on the air. The others noticed it too. Then Ron explained.

'You silly fuckers. That great horrible place across the way there's a fucking abbattoir. What d'ye expect?'

All day they laboured in the heat, hating the smell which thickened and corrupted the air. At noon they clambered up on to the pile of chippings to dig themselves hollows in which to sit and eat their sandwiches. But as they unscrewed their flasks of tea and opened the greaseproof paper to inspect the contents of the sandwiches their wives had made, they seemed to suffer a collective loss of appetite. The paper packages were crumpled up and only the tea was drunk. Soon they were back at work, driving their barrows faster and faster, loading them competitively higher and higher, knowing that the faster they worked the sooner they could escape this tainted air.

High up on the stone wall edging a market in Istanbul a yellow bird trilled from a fragile cage. No-one seemed to listen. The cruelty was routine, of no account. Better to hear the tiny wren, its song out of all proportion to its size, or the midnight cry of owls (hunting the mouse more savagely than any taut trap set on a kitchen's quarry tiles), or the song of a robin redbreast perched on the handle of a spade, than the cry of a caged bird. The squirrel slithering down a tree, the rabbit munching wet grass at dawn by the side of a lane, the cautious fox throwing a quick, shrewd glance from the far side of a field before disappearing through a practised gap in the hedge. Better to see these creatures free and uncontained, as we would wish to be, without collars and leads and bells and cages and kennels. *They treated them like animals. I wouldn't have given that to a dog.* But there is no act of human degradation that has not yet been thought of and implemented. Outside the camps and torture cells, the birds are free, singing, in flight, past the bars, out of sight and sound of the screams of humans practising their cruelty on each other.

If we do not love the creatures (yes, yes, amongst themselves they are red in tooth and claw) can we love ourselves? If we let hate in are we squeezing out the possibility of love? How much room is there in the human heart?

# 33. THE LOVE OF ONESELF

'TO LOVE ONESELF,' announced the great Oscar – in his high phase of fame before he sat, crumpled between two prison guards, on the platform at Clapham Junction, society having exacted its payment at last for the years of having hosted his subversive wit – 'is the beginning of a lifelong romance.' The self-righteous shudder at the selfishness of the man, a charge, however, which he had anticipated (one more quote only, for once started on Oscar one might fill a book): 'Selfishness is not living as one wishes to live. It is asking other people to live as one wishes to live.' From the man who wrote the only joyous socialist tract in English, who knew that the soul as well as the body needs a reward, to be given a fruitful task to perform on the great collective farm of social justice (alas, the puritans took over and the rest is a dreary history of righteousness and speeches in draughty halls) came these quick bright arrows of wit to pierce the thick carapace of Victorian England. To juggle *gravitas* and levity (a habitual process in the city of Felix and his father); to see them dance within the confines of the same sentence, shining light on each other's faces, discovering, in the heart of each, a depth previously unknown, is rarer than it ought to be. For which, gratitude is due to Mr Wilde.

But the self? Amid the din of Self-Assertiveness courses, the Freudian pithead wheel, hauling up cages of precious material from the depths below, the clamour of sectional interests asserting special rights and titles, who would dare say that the self is dust, blown particles of sand? Marcel Proust, it is said, compared himself to a flea.

Perhaps we are nothing, insignificant as stone in a river bed, the dry twig ignored by the foraging rodent, unseen patterns of frost on the window of an abandoned shooting-lodge on a November dawn. I think not. The insistent self is never so effacing. It will never tolerate such an eclipse.

Narcissus, son of the river-nymph Liriope (product of a brutal riverine rape by the flowing god Cephisus – but this is too much to have to remember) was noticed in his cradle by the seer Tiresias who prophesied that he would live to a ripe old age 'if he does not come to know himself'. More beautiful than any teen-idol, the despair of the opposite sex, Narcissus – walled around with pride and self-love – wandered the countryside alone. Feeling that it mattered above all else to know himself (ignorant of the simple fact that it is through knowing others that we attain that particular knowledge) Narcissus cut himself off from the maidens who would willingly have thrown themselves on him (however much we might disapprove on feminist grounds of such behaviour). He wandered up hill and down vale, until he was noticed by the beautiful nymph, Echo. [Her present predicament of being able to speak only in the form of returning the words just spoken by others came about – you will recall – from her former habit of detaining the goddess Juno with small talk. This was to allow her fellow-nymphs, with whom Juno's husband Jupiter had been philandering, to escape.] Echo was, it goes without saying, immediately smitten but all she could do was parrot the end of another person's sentences which – although more common in the speech of lovers than of normal citizens – was not entirely helpful in these circumstances. So she was ignored by Narcissus, who found a clear pool, shielded from the heat of the sun by tall reeds, and gazed lovingly at the image he saw reflected there. It seemed to him that here was the most beautiful form he could ever wish to see, the one that truly matched up to his own expectations, that overcame the inadequacies and fallings-short of all the potential lovers who had thrust themselves in his path. No-one else could be so pleasing to him. Yet at the same time, when he reached out to embrace this paragon, the image vanished in a ripple and splash of water, and he found himself clutching pond-weed and empty air. Things got no better, as they seldom do for those who cannot achieve their object of desire, and Narcissus, pining by his pool, grew pale and anorexic and slowly wasted away. When they came to lift him on to his funeral pyre the body had vanished and in its place was a circle of pale narcissi.

A moral, Reverend, a conclusion, Doctor. The Greeks concluded that this was a triumph for the foresight of Tiresias. Echo retreated to the depths of a dark cave where she can still be heard and as a result of which the work of lexicographers can briefly be brightened. And we have a name for self-love, for the long romance with the wrong object, for the error of thinking that we matter too much when in reality it can often seem that we do not matter at all. Putting oneself aside, forgetting the perfections one sees in one's own reflection, one might begin to notice – in the busy street outside the prison of the self – the noise and hubbub made by other people and start to practise the after-you and don't-mention-its of the world.

## 34. THE LOST GIRL

IN THE CITY of Turin there is a restaurant called *La Smarrita* which is translated for the occasional foreign visitor as *The Lost Girl*. No more is said. Fumbling with his limited grasp of the language, the literate Englishman remembers that opening canto of Dante's Inferno he once got by heart.

> *Nel mezzo del cammin di nostra vita*
> *mi ritrovai per una selva oscura*
> *che la diritta via era smarrita.*

To be lost, in Dante's Christian allegory, is to have mislaid one's moral bearings, to be in a state of unknowing about one's purposes in life. And this at the time of life when such questions ought to have been determined, the deal struck, the contract signed. If we do not know ourselves at the halfway point of a life, will we ever do so? It is a nice idea, befitting a world view where all is settled, where the pieces fit together with a satisfying click. But the man or woman who reads Dante today is sitting in a different library chair. Uncertainty for the gravid philosopher, the daily wrestle with trivia for the rest of us, have put paid to this. We are all in a place where the dark wood has been felled and replaced by a tangle of fast freeways lit by bright lights. One can choose any lane or exit but to select a destination has become the most difficult thing. In many cases it is not even desired.

Was it a philosopher or a whimsical Romantic who named this restaurant? One enters late from the theatre, ascending to the first floor up a magnificent baroque staircase – the whole building prodigal of space, a certain easy, languid elegance its keynote. The waiters are courteous but unfussy, the restaurant lacks the insistent decor, the announced theme, the importunate semiotics, of the fashionable restaurant in London or New York. Mercifully, the designers have not been allowed at it.

There is a table by the window. Some dry white wine is brought. A little later the waiters arrive with a silver dish of delicious ravioli which they scoop deftly on to small plates to whet the appetite. Suddenly a crowd appears at the door to be greeted warmly by the *padrone*. They are excited, self-contained, acknowledging glances and subdued greetings from several tables. They are the cast of a Chekhov play which has just played its last night.

Who was the lost girl? Did she choose this night to leave without a forwarding address? Was she perhaps merely glimpsed, covertly, in a corner of the restaurant where she sat by herself, picking at a pale tangle of *fettucini*, a glass of wine untouched? Perhaps the owner, aching with desire for a woman whom he would never be allowed to know, named his restaurant as a public declaration of his despair. The patron on a first visit entertains all these speculations and cannot rid himself of the image of a beautiful young woman, pausing on the steps of the restaurant, then rushing away, her heels clattering across the flagstones of the nearby square, spurred on by some secret distress. Perhaps too, there is the fleeting image of Daphne, Apollo hot on her heels, the god who must have everything and everyone, chasing her until her body flowers into the laurel tree, foiling his lust with peremptory vegetation. In this stolid town of the Italian north, where the citizens walk their substantial arcades, in green overcoats and ochre hats with a feather in the band, it is good to see a gesture to the unstolid world of love, that fluid element in which we so often swim to safety

– or towards the safety of risk.

The lost girl should be let go. She should not be pursued even if the ache goes on throughout a lifetime, crossing the *mezzo del cammin*, and haunting the silent, self-communing inner spaces of old age. Let go, let her go, let her run across the midnight flagstones, do not stop her like a jealous god who would freeze her into the shape of a tree or a rock or a fountain spilling its water into a remote pool. Her freedom is your freedom. To arrest her, to invade her wish, her right to escape, would be to enslave yourself. A love that insists, that presses itself against resistance, will result in a world of lost girls, running across the vast, rain-soaked, moonlight-reflecting square, running to retrieve themselves, running to regain their freedom to love in their own way and at their own rate.

Let her go. *La smarrita* of our youth. Irretrievable. Lost.

# 35. LOVE'S DECEITS

LOVERS ARE THEIR own legislators. They make up their own rules and tear up the rule book of others. Happily, they are always in the right. Their desires are the law. All's fair.

Goaded by his jealous courtiers, who whispered in his ear sly warnings about the amorous activities of Tristan (whom they loathed as an usurper of influence and position), King Mark of Cornwall grew angry with the man who had saved his country's bacon by slaying the Morholt. Enter the wicked dwarf, Frocin, who knew from the exercise of his dark magic the secret of the lovers. He knew that Tristan would come at night into the orchard that grew around the castle at Tintagel where Iseut slept (or did not sleep). Iseut would gaze down from her window on the stream that gurgled through the orchard below. When she saw floating on its surface the twigs that Tristan had cut she knew that he was in the orchard and waiting for her. Frocin, by dint of his magic, knew this too. He advised the King to conceal himself in an apple-tree above the stream where he would learn everything he needed to know about the perfidy of the lovers. This was in the early days of their illicit love, before the days of their madness and separation. That night, the two lovers approached each other eagerly but Iseut caught sight of a strange reflection in the moonlit surface of the water. She realised that there was a figure hiding in the tree above the water and that it could be none other than her husband. Putting on a bold voice, she reprimanded Tristan (who by now had also glimpsed the figure on the surface of the stream and caught her drift). For all his good looks and accomplishments and courage and manliness...

'Please!'

'It's just a word, Trish.'

'How can you say that as a writer? Only words. They are your building blocks, your meaning. If words are only words why should we pay them any heed? Sometimes I think all we have is words. Tell me something that can be achieved without words, that lives outside language.'

'Point taken.'

I meant to say that Tristan, like some Hollywood idol, had all the right qualities for a macho star but when it came to intelligence, shrewdness, *savoir-faire*, Iseut left him standing by the stream. She was seriously smart. Entering into her role as an outraged and virtuous wife, she hammed it up for all she was worth for the benefit of the man in the tree. This gave Tristan enough time to understand the game sufficiently to respond in kind. She insisted that the gossip was unfounded and malicious – as they both knew – and that no-one had ever enjoyed her bed except the man who had taken her as a virgin. This was a very subtle touch.

'Meaning?'

She spoke no less than the truth because on her wedding night (by which time she and Tristan had more than adequately resolved the question of her maidenhood) King Mark had been duped. The doggedly loyal Brangain – who had not let her employer-employee relationship be affected by her mistress's earlier attempt to have her assassinated in a dark wood so she wouldn't blab – had been roped in to a clever deception to get round the fact of Iseut's being no longer a maiden. This is what happened: on the wedding night, Tristan had steered King Mark into the bedchamber where all the lights had been put out.

'Why have the candles been snuffed, Sir Tristan?' asked the King.

'Oh, it's an old Irish custom,' replied Tristan. 'It'll make Iseut feel at home. As you can imagine, she'll be a bag of nerves.'

To ram the point home he jabbed the King in the ribs and leered. 'Fair enough,' said the monarch as he went off to brush his teeth. Iseut quickly hopped out of bed and scampered out of the room through a side door while Brangain took her place between the sheets. When, some time later, they heard the satisfied snores of the King, Iseut and Tristan crept in to the room and hauled Brangain out of bed, installing Iseut back in her place. As can be imagined, they felt very smug at the success of their little game. So when Iseut claimed that she had only ever been with the man who had taken her as a virgin she at one and the same time spoke the truth and convinced the husband in the apple tree that she was the most virtuous and honest woman in Cornwall.

Once they had decided the playacting had created the desired effect, the lovers went their separate ways and the King shinned down the tree, determined to catch hold of the little hunch-backed dwarf and wring his neck. Frocin, however (by virtue of his gift of divination) got the astral message that the King was on the warpath and immediately decamped in the direction of Wales. It was thought that he would never be seen again.

Brangain and Iseut, together with Tristan and his personal assistant Gorvenal, all got together to compare notes and congratulate themselves on the way they had hoodwinked the King. Brangain even suggested that God had been on their side. 'He is a true father, and He will not harm those who are loyal and good,' she observed, which was rather going beyond the mark. The King then sent for them all and made an apology but Tristan (rather too pleased with himself for his trickery) pretended to be outraged and demanded a stronger apology for the base accusations that had been made against him. The King duly grovelled to his nephew who told him haughtily that he should henceforth take better advice, steer clear of malicious dwarfs, and treat the virtuous Queen and the unimpeachable Tristan with proper respect. 'Tristan, make yourself at home in my chamber whenever you like,' said the King. Tristan bowed gracefully at this, trying not to catch Iseut's eye.

And so the bare-faced cheek of the lovers triumphed. They had lied, cheated and pretended that God was on their side throughout. And they had got away with it. All in all a typical night's work for a pair of illicit lovers.

And – have you noticed? – every reader is on their side.

# 36. THE LOVE OF BOOKS

BIBLIOPHILIA. THE WORST kind of madness. 'Every science,' writes Georg Wilhelm Friedrich Hegel in his *Introductory Lectures on Aesthetics*, 'has the prerogative of marking out its boundaries at pleasure.' The bibliophile knows that there are two categories of obsession which might be labelled for convenience, form and content. As in the ponderous gropings of aesthetic philosophers who would separate artistic form from artistic meaning – an activity as absurd as attempting to separate the colour from the scent of the rose – we are in love with these phantom apparitions, pairing like couples at a dance, separating and rejoining to whirl down the sawdust-strewn floor as the gypsy fiddler savagely saws at his violin. It is possible to use the words, to persuade ourselves that there is a distinction here. Form and content. But what work of art could ever be diced in two? For the content is form and the form is content. What this thing means lies in the way it is said and done. The moralists will object that art has a purpose – to elevate, to educate, to change the world. These purposes may be ancillary – at certain times of the day one might be disposed to endorse them – but all art must cherish its element of the gratuitous. In its freedom resides its value, in its absence of purposeful logic its most forceful meaning.

So the bibliophile, the abject lover of the book, knows that there is the text, the printed gateway to meaning, the spirit lodged briefly in actual substance. And there is the palpable casing, the physical object that may be handled, swung from a shelf, caressed, tossed away in disgust. His or her detractor will seize on the delinquency of book-lust, its cardinal error:

to mistake the thing for the idea, to commit the first folly that will lead, in the course of time, to the inferno of fine bindings.

They called him The Rubber Man.

It is a sunny morning in the tiny market town. The summer season of visitors is almost begun. Cyril, whose shop boasts *NO REPRODUCTION ITEMS EVER KNOWINGLY SOLD*, a proposition crisply refuted by the contents of his shop-window, is setting out his boxes and clutter of objects: a ceramic chamber pot, a pitted beech-wood rolling-pin, a shaky tower of black vinyl gramophone records, a rusty cylindrical lawn-mower, a gate-legged table in need of serious refurbishment, a wooden box in which are jumbled old woodworking tools (spokeshave, adze, box plane), a Gladstone bag, a suitcase overflowing with books, warped and stained from exposure to the wind and rain.

Inside the shop are the finer items, the porcelain and the bentwood chairs, the fine bindings and the works of local topography. In the back rooms are the stacks of books-worth-looking-after where The Rubber Man does his work.

Out inspecting a house being cleared, or travelling back from a rough outdoor sale held in the early hours, Cyril's absence was filled by his occasional deputy, Christopher. The Rubber Man chooses his moment carefully. Pausing to inspect the illustrated cover of an Edwardian book of popular music scores, he casts a quick, shrewd glance through the window, long enough to notice Christopher with a mug of tea and a copy of *The Daily Express* spread out on the counter. The door opens stiffly. The bell shivers. Christopher looks up.

'Nice morning.'

'It's supposed to rain later on.'

'As long as my boss doesn't get a soaking.'

A short, nervous laugh and The Rubber Man is already at work, going straight to the sections on topography, natural history, collecting, clocks, bell ringing, trams – in short, all those subjects which that great friend of the true bibliomane, the incomparable Driffield, categorises (in his masterful work on the business of hunting the used book and prising it out of the hands of its reluctant and often discourteous custodians) as 'roast beef'. While Christopher bends down to discover what is in store for those born under the sign of Scorpio, The Rubber Man strikes. Leafing back through the pages of Winstanley's *History of the County of R-*, he finds the pencilled '£35' where he knew it would be. Steadily, unfussily, he draws from his pocket a narrow, hard green rubber eraser and, with a quick, deft, practised movement, strikes out the digit '3' with four or five rapid up-and-down strokes, brushing away the crumbs of rubber with his sleeve.

'Thank you, Sir, how much is that?' Christopher asks the customer, as if his natural dignity precluded him from possessing the vulgar knowledge of his stock of a mere tradesman. The Rubber Man enters into the charade, playing the part of the befuddled innocent. Christopher, as if noticing the book for the first time, strokes its spine as one might a well-groomed horse at a five-barred gate at the edge of a field.

'That looks a very nice book. Does it say five pounds?'

The Rubber Man obligingly stoops. He flaunts his myopia. He concurs in the stated price. No, he does not need a bag. Goodbye. Yes, it does look like rain after such a promising start. Cheerio. As he hurries down the High Street why does he show no pleasure at his acquisition?

Later, Cyril will return. The shop will echo with loud words of protest and exasperation. Recrimination will fence against wounded self-justification. The rain will hurl itself against the window of the shop and the weather will be bad for trade.

# 37. FAZAKERLEY

THE POET KEATS was half in love with easeful death. Outside the brilliantly lit chamber of the poem, in what sentimentalists call The Real World, it is hard to see why anyone would pine for extinction. Quite apart from the issue of pain, the altruism of sparing the grief of one's friends, there is the question of not wanting it to finish quite yet, of there being still business to be done.

Felix was at an age when others might consider themselves middle-aged, when the sense came, not of impending death but of having reached a plateau in a life, a point of rest where there was more surveying of the view than fashioning it to be done. That was the possibility. The temptation. The mediaeval philosopher Isidore of Seville did not share our modern parcelling up of the human life-cycle. The child, according to Isidore, from birth to the age of six was in a state of infancy. Childhood ran from seven to thirteen, adolescence from fourteen to twenty-seven, youth from twenty-eight to forty-eight, and – most interesting of all – maturity began at forty-nine and ran to seventy-six. Old age was finally permitted at seventy-seven. And after age the only end of age. Felix approved. He looked forward to the imminent state of maturity, an envied state almost as tempting as youth and as far as both from the ante-room of death. His had been a life of deferred hopes, of endless new beginnings, of refusals, of resistances to the notion of finding a fixed point, a reliable berth. He sought trouble, he sought flux, he loved violent discontinuities, not the comfort of habit and routine. In this way he surprised his friends who saw an outward quietness in the tenor of his life, who were surprised when the occasional actual rupture broke through. But he had always been bad at appearances, at tapping out the appropriate signals. To sum up: death was not welcome, whether sickly-sweet and Keatsian, or violent and ugly.

In the depths of his despair, that peculiar despair that tortures those who have seen their own minds slipping away to conspire against themselves; in the dark hours that could have made a Felix into a Tristan, howling in bleak, intransitive madness, he never longed for death, he always believed in life, he was a hope-junkie. Mornings of autumn where ineffable skies and frost-melting sunlight sent out a trumpet-call of exaltation, any species of beginning or expectancy – the first page of a book, the start of a journey, the arrival of someone or some adventure – transformed and delighted him. At those moments life was quickened. Perhaps too it was understood.

But death was a cancellation of hope. He would accept it when it came, with good grace. He might even consider doing it in style, acting the part of a wise stoic, conceding that the time was right, the accounts paid, all loose ends gathered up.

In the city they pronounced the name that sounded like Nemesis. The bright hospital with its belt of crowded carparks. Fazakerley. The name that would stalk them. And when they came there for the last time, speechless on their white beds, surrounded by the pious murmuring, the mechanical reassurances, the fraudulent hopes of people in flying, ball-point-scratched white coats, and of their 'loved ones' whom they could no longer hear or cast on the screen of their damaged inward sight, Fazakerley would have notched up another success, added another trophy to his belt.

Far better to hope. To keep on hoping. To remain in love with beginnings rather than with endings.

# 38. OF LUCRE

WHAT IS IT, in the end – to the miser, to the broker, to the international banker, to the child with its porcelain pig, to the bookie at the race track, to the global entrepreneur – but a row of noughts? Even to a world that has replaced the love of God with the love of shopping, whose wayside pulpit is an advertising billboard, it must often be a disappointment. Once, there was the satisfying chink and tinkle of gold coins, the gleam in the crock. Now there is plastic and PINs, and the sad, far-off bleating sound of the Little Englanders lamenting for their poor pound, stolen in the night by Europeans with droopy moustaches, black berets, and garlic breath. How, in all conscience, can one be in love with a balance sheet?

But try telling that to the poor. In truth you have to be rich to afford the luxury of despising wealth. Have you noticed how the rich love the very idea of poverty? The richer they are the more they glamorise their days of being poor before hard graft – for which read inherited capital, the lucky break – put them where they are, their arses on the plush of posh hotels (have you noticed, by the bye, the stupefying *vulgarity* of the world's most expensive hotels?), their lives attended to by people whose services they have bought and continue to buy. They take a special pleasure in the sight of beggars slumped in the doorways as they emerge from the restaurant. It's a sort of validation. It makes sense of being rich.

So we're agreed, then, the love of money is the greatest of all the *amours fous*? You ask: how much am I getting paid for this?

# 39. SKIP

POLITICIANS, CHURCHMEN, SENTIMENTALISTS, are all agreed. The question is wrapped up. No doubt about it. The one rock on which society is built. The family. True, there are occasional dysfunctions – the home life of Frederick and Rosemary West was, of course, *of course*, an example of... well, dysfunction. But let's not allow one suppurating cox pippin to get away with securing a conviction of the whole damned barrel.

Fathers and sons, mothers and daughters, brothers and sisters. We still haven't got to Grandma and a whole heap of business for the therapists has already piled up. 'The dysfunctional family,' a psychotherapist observed to Felix (who was pressed up against the wall of a tiled kitchen, his fingers having crushed the fluted wall of a plastic cup of lukewarm tinned beer, a piece of spinach quiche gripped, half eaten, in his other hand) 'is the typical family.' As the world, slowly, with a pained grimace, peels back the carpet to reveal the scuttling family of cockroaches beneath, it is tempting to look the other way, to let the carpet fall back with a dusty slap. Abuse. Physical, psychological, sexual.

Oh, come, come. It has Always Been Like This. Strange things have gone on between the sheets, behind the locked door of Number Fourteen. Who hasn't a tale to tell? Don't we all just hitch up our skirts and ford forward through the mud? Too much self-pity, too much whingeing, too much craving for martyrdom. All those whining, victimy persons crowding into the courtrooms with their miraculously recovered memories. Abuse. An abuse of credulity, I call it.

Thank you, madam. Thank you for that contribution.

Felix joined the Boy Scouts. The ghost of Baden Powell, the flinty Imperialist, the advocate of cold showers, and a jug of cold tap water to fend off lust, who told you how to hear the sound of distant horses approaching (since you ask, a twin-bladed penknife, one blade thrust in the good earth of the veldt, the other clamped between one's teeth), whose Boer War skills were transposed, absurdly, to English suburbia, would have let out a pained howl of anguish had it flitted down to witness the troop of Sea Scouts into which Felix enlisted.

Harry Kirkdale, the skipper of this dishevelled crew, stood at the top end of the meeting room with its thick brown linoleum and bare walls, in his blue serge shorts from which protruded a pair of knobbly knees, his withered arm tucked into his left trouser pocket. Skip commanded his patrols (Felix in charge of The Seagull platoon) with a weak – or perhaps an indifferent – authority. He seemed always to be waiting for the moment when they could be dismissed for periods of separate activity in the scattered rooms of this large, decaying old house that had once been the family home. He retreated into his study where it was a study to see him uncap a grey fountain pen with his teeth. He should have been signing certificates of proficiency – in the tying of knots, the basic procedures of First Aid, the techniques of seamanship – but he preferred to let the boys run wild, for which they were always properly grateful.

Skip had the look of an old sea dog – with his short grizzled grey beard, pointed like King Edward VI on the back of the penny coin, and with that roguish twinkle in his eye. In fact he had ventured no further than the Seacombe ferry and worked as a shipping clerk in the tall buildings by the waterfront capped by a flight of greenish copper cormorants.

Sometimes Skip took the boys sailing in a thick, heavy tub of a sailing dinghy which was launched from a timber slipway at a muddy estuary a few miles north of the decadent house. Sleek racing dinghies with laughing crewmen in bright waterproofs throwing out derisive gestures shot past the floundering Sea Scouts in their comical tub as the tide rose and Skip shouted in a shrill voice to one of the boys: 'Get the plate up, James! Get the plate up!'

After one such voyage, after sandwiches and green pop in the clubhouse, Felix travelled back with Skip on the electric railway through the dunes. The gentle clerk, with his twinkling eye and his vestigial arm tucked into the pocket of a navy blue gaberdine, spoke to Felix but ignored him. He wittered inconsequentially. A soft burble of confused recollection of his childhood, of his family, that glassed his eye and sent it staring out of the window of the train – as if some aid to reflection or recall would come from the grey sky, the wild golf-course, or the marram-tipped dunes – trickled out throughout the whole journey.

Felix walked back with him from the station. Skip consulted his watch nervously. He explained that his sisters would be waiting for him, that they would expect him not to be late. When they reached the front gate of his quiet house with its green lawn in front, Felix watched him go, along the narrow pathway of stone flags between the neat lozenges of cropped and rolled grass. A lace curtain moved in the corner of the bay window. His sister opened the door and smiled, drawing him in to that quiet interior no scout had ever intruded upon.

She drew the wistful bachelor-clerk, once again, back into the gentle province of her love.

# 40. ON BEING FOUND OUT

THE CABINET MINISTER on the dark common. The clergyman tumbled out of his love nest. The public figure stalked by the *paparazzi*. The victim phoned on Saturday afternoon by the tabloid newspaper to warn of 'allegations' in the next morning's edition. What do they do? They do what all human beings do. They lie through their teeth. The point about certain kinds of love – often the most passionate, often the most absolute – is that they want to take place in secret. They don't want to be found out. But there are always those who want to do the finding out and publish the results. And to do so from a pulpit.

Tristan and Iseut, for example, who successfully tricked the King of Cornwall with all that business below a tree, were not so successful with the moral vigilantes. The happily deceived King received a visit from a party of knights who were determined to open the royal eyes to the goings-on. Three in particular appointed themselves as Special Prosecutors and paid the King a visit. They told him that, whatever the King might think, and whatever Tristan's approval ratings were with the Cornish public, an illicit affair was going on. It was no use listening to Tristan's denials. They would furnish proof after which he would have no option but to send the over-lusty knight packing. For the Special Prosecutors had seen the two lovers in various compromising situations. They had even – according to the chroniclers of the legend – seen the couple lying naked together (the Cornish knights being accomplished voyeurs or scopophiliacs). But these titled Peeping-Toms needed some decisive proof to lay before the gullible King. In short, they needed the prophetic dwarf, Frocin, now rehabilitated after the tryst-under-the-tree fiasco. Frocin was just the man for the job. He had the Puritan's vengeful lust to gaze on every last graphic detail of Sin. He wanted to know every sexual position, every act, every lubricious word and deed, and when there was nothing left to hear then he wanted to string the perpetrators up. Frocin was a small-town guy who had made it to court and was determined to nail Tristan to the floor for being so handsome and so powerful and so brave. So far so good.

So trusting was the King in the wake of his experiences up the tree that he allowed Tristan to sleep in his own bedchamber, only a few feet from the royal resting-place itself. From this handy berth Tristan, as one might expect, made various nocturnal excursions. Frocin's plan was as follows. He went to a baker and bought several bags of flour which, after lights out, he scattered on the floor of the bedchamber between the two beds. It so happened that Tristan had sustained a rather nasty injury from hunting wild boar that day. The pain kept him awake. In a shaft of moonlight he noticed that the floor was covered in white flour. Being rather quick on the uptake – though never as sharp as Iseut – he realised that someone was setting a trap. So when the King rose and went outside to join the Special Prosecutors, by whom he had been told that this would catch the blighter, Tristan took care not to leave his tell-tale footprints all over the bedchamber floor. Instead, he leaped over the trap and landed on Iseut's bed where, notwithstanding the painful wound, he proceeded to do what it is not necessary, unless one is a Special Prosecutor, to itemise. When he had finished, he made another Tristan's Leap back into his own bed. The trick might have worked but for that boar-goring. Not only was the royal bed drenched in Tristan's blood but tell-tale drops lay on the white sheet of flour, so that the most thick-witted investigator could work out the trajectory of the leap. At this point the door burst open and the King, the three Special Prosecutors, and the sniggering dwarf Frocin bounded into the room, grabbing Tristan by the collar of his nightshirt. One of the three, who had watched too many cop-shows, even shouted out in his excitement: 'You're nicked!' This time there was no escape, no excuses, no clever deceptions, and Tristan was taken away, charged, and sentenced. But he escaped on the way to his execution by leaping over the Cornish cliffs – but that's another story and you've heard it already.

Should lovers be found out? Should we be told? Should the whole world come trooping into the bedroom with its notebooks and videorecorders to ask what happened and who did what to whom? In Underground compartments, in dentists' waiting rooms, on sunny Indian summer park-benches, in Turkish tea houses, and Chinese marketplaces, the world – which had nothing better to do at the time – read the neat printed handwriting of the President's mistress: *A little phrase (with only eight letters) like 'thank you' simply cannot begin to express what I feel you have given me. Art and poetry are gifts to my soul!* Should we feel sorry for this young woman? Should we feel sorry for Mr President? Whom should we blame? Him? Her? Neither? Perhaps ourselves?

*Handsome, you have been distant the past few months and have shut me out: I don't know why. Is it that you don't like me any more or are you scared?*

Oh yes, we all have a view on this. Like chin-stroking farmers at a cattle market, or literary critics sidling up to a text with twisted, disapproving faces, we all know what to say. Poor girl, little hussy, pathetic tart, pathetic old man, couldn't keep his dog in the porch, why did he give her a copy of Whitman's *Leaves of Grass*? And all the people in glass-houses picked up stones to throw at the pair of them, as if none of them knew what this was, as if none had ever got themselves into this pickle and lied to get themselves out of it. As if a reflection in the moonlight or a carpet of white flour hadn't alerted them to the possibility that this wasn't meant to be and that they had better start being inventive. For when you are in love and you shouldn't be the rule is not be found out and from this flows all the mess and the complications and the unfortunately-I-had-to-work-lates and the little things that will later hurt so much. But people go on thinking that they can leap that oblong of white flour. And they go on forgetting that a few drops of blood might fall. For when you are in love you can't think of everything because most of the time you are thinking of just one thing.

But whether this is something called Tragedy or whether it is something else I leave you to decide.

# 41. OF NATURE

THE PHILOSOPHER HEGEL said that the beauty of Art was higher than the beauty of Nature. That's philosophers for you. Always suggesting that something is 'higher' than something else. By art, he meant sculpture and poetry and painting and literature. What he called fine art – *schöne Kunst*. His argument was that the beauty of art is born out of the mind whereas the beauty of, let us say, the streams and stones and arching trees of the Forest of Morroiz is just there, without the human intelligence having much to do with it one way or the other.

*And by as much as the mind and its products are higher than nature and its appearances, by so much the beauty of art is higher than the beauty of nature.*

Try telling that to Wordsworth.

He even argued that a daft thought flitting through the brain was worth more than a fine sunset because it was *characterised by intellectual being and by freedom*.

Felix went out from the old-fashioned hotel, which lay just beyond the far end of the quietest of the Lakes, on his first outing of exploration. He paused by the road where five milk-churns stood on a stout wooden platform then crossed over to the still dewy grassy track that turned left, crossing an arched stone bridge. He looked down into the pure, swiftly-flowing water and thought he saw the silvery flash of a small fish. He knew the word stickleback but had no idea how to identify one of these creatures mentioned in a book. Perhaps he could find a fishing-rod or a line and catch one. Some people in the hotel last night had said that they had picked the fruit that had been used in the pie. Perhaps he could bring back a fish for the cook to prepare so that when the great big gong in the gloomy hall was beaten and everyone trooped into the dining-room they would point to the fish on its oval plate and say that he had caught it in the stream or out on the Lake.

From the bridge, the track ran straight down to the Lake then started to follow its edge. There were large flat cow-droppings on the grass, like shrivelled-up pancakes, and big stones lay scattered around. Felix pulled at one until he was able to raise it up. Underneath was a fat, glossy black slug with twitching antennae. He let the stone drop with a sudden YUK! He looked around at the wet grass, the wind rippling the surface of the Lake, the hills behind with their purple carpets of heather, and he sniffed the breeze. It was cold and clean and fresh like the river and the grass and the rippling water and it was as if he was noticing for the first time in his life the purity and the cleanness of air and water, as if this was the first time and at the same time the beginning of its end for nothing ever again could seem as clear and as beautiful and as tangy as the air of that morning by the Lake.

## 42. THE LOVE OF FREEDOM

LIKE TRUTH – another hefty abstraction that demands to be addressed in the full livery of its initial capital – Freedom is one of the great passions of humankind. And here is another: the love of exercising power, of curtailing freedom, of snuffing it out like a candle-flame between a great big greasy finger and thumb, of announcing that freedom is a delusion and that obedience is a virtue. These are the people (in religious rigout, in military uniforms jangling with rows of medals, with swagger sticks and truncheons and electric prods) who argue that freedom is the enemy, that freedom is the cause of all the trouble in the world. Such people have a glint in their eye which is like a sliver of ice in the heart. They will send a mob to tear a house and its inhabitants apart. They will cry for books to be banned because they give Offence, forgetting that offence is taken as well as given, that some people need to be offended, to have their noses rubbed in the crushed petals of freedom, to know what a world of open spirits rather than a world of closed spirits might be like.

At an upper window, the dictator looks down on the parade ground, at the goose-stepping conscripts marching in rows, and thinks of his power, his power to crush, to bring down, to clear a space for the strutting vacancy of himself, his cold, monumental public artworks and martial bronzes. What society needs is a good thrashing. The taste for freedom needs to be extinguished, rooted out. It is a bad addiction that must not be allowed to corrupt the purity of youth.

Perhaps the hatred of freedom is the hatred of oneself.

The angry patriarch thumping the kitchen table, the

husband howling at his cowering wife, the religious funda-
mentalist intoning his list of forbidden books, the newspaper
columnist saying: enough-is-enough. They are frightened of
themselves, they are frightened of the freedom that they
might find there, coursing through their veins like a virus,
troubling their certainties. For freedom – which is sometimes made to sound like fun, like something naughty, like a
bit of a lark – is in fact harder than it looks, for the free-from
are free-to. And being free-to isn't always an easy option. No
wonder so many prefer to hide behind the skirts of the dictators and the rule-makers and the ones who slap their
swagger sticks against their khaki thighs.

The dictator looks over the heads of the marching
platoons, across the high wall of the parade ground, and lifts
his eyes to the bright morning sky where a gull soars across
the blueness like a distant jet leaving a vapour trail. Buoyed
up on currents of air, bright against that unflecked blue, the
gull is free. Does this irk him? Does he wish that he had a
powerful rifle in his hand to take aim and bring it down? Or
does the sliver of ice in his heart look for a moment as
though it might melt? Hate makes a man or woman lonely,
trapped in the cold tower of self, the prison island where the
cry of gulls is heard as they swoop down to shores where
breakers crash, heard but not seen by the chained inmates.
Hate is a terrible ball and chain, a terrible constriction. It
takes the heart and squeezes it dry. It makes the whole of life
a prison island, a dripping cell where no visitors come and
where it is always night.

# 43. THE BADGE

LOGOPHILIA. GLOSSOLALIA. The words that define the love of language, the gift of tongues, are themselves unlovely. But who is not in love with words, their sounds and shapes, the way they slip from the tongue like melting ice or stay there, chewy and resistant, like gristle? Long words, short words, words that get us into trouble. Words that get us out of trouble. Words that want to say much more than they can, words which fear they have said too much. Words which hurt and words which heal. Words that seem to take all our love or hate. Words that try to build bridges between people and words which smash them down.

But the love of language is more than the love of words, piled up like stones on a mountain cairn. Language is not words, it is the spaces between words, the patterns words form, the things that they do. Sometimes it is even silence, saying nothing. The autodidact who swallows the dictionary, learning ten new words a day, is not wasting time but may be missing the point. But the man who invented the science of linguistics, and who said that language was an arbitrary system of signs, was, like most thinkers, only half right.

For Saussure language was like a chess-game going on in one of the turrets of King Mark's castle at Tintagel. The fire was blazing in the grate, the two players, seated on opposite sides of a beautiful ivory chessboard, were surrounded by ten knights and ladies. The arras was rippling softly in the draught because twelfth century castles had no idea about insulation. Then it was discovered that a pawn was missing from the box. The players were forced to improvise with an upturned acorn cup. Provided all twelve people in the room agreed that an upside-down acorn cup was a pawn that was enough. The shape and size was arbitrary so long as everyone understood that it had been assigned the meaning of 'pawn'. But of course this theory is not quite good enough. It is not good enough for poets and artists who can see a difference between an acorn cup or a bottle-top or a salt-cellar and a carved ivory pawn in the shape of a Cornish foot-soldier, ranged with his fellows in front of knights on horseback, splendid bishops, imposing castles, and the great monarch and his consort. They look at the folds of his armour, the lance defiantly lifted, the fierce courage that the sculptor's tiny knife has carved on the eight faces which stare across the no-man's land of unoccupied black and white squares and they say: no, let us not make a fetish of words but let us also remember that language is more than a system, more than the squiggly soldering and circuitry and microchips of a computer's motherboard.

Felix's father was in love with language, the proof being the badge he made that day.

Towards the end of the 1950s, when the 1960s (which no-one could have predicted) were just getting ready to start, the Lord Mayor, and the councillors and the planners, decided that something must be done about the narrow streets and tenements and squares of the city where the poor people lived. As is usually the case in these situations someone came up with a bright idea and because no-one could think of a better idea they seized on this one with frenzy, slapping the inventor on the back and telling each other that this was the best idea that anyone had ever come up with. The idea was called Overspill.

Losing no time, the Lord Mayor planned a special ceremony to celebrate the invention of Overspill. Everyone gathered at the town hall and cheered madly as the Lord Mayor stepped forward to open the brass tap that would release the first few gallons of Overspill. But something quite unexpected happened. The tap came off in the Lord Mayor's hand and instead of a trickle out came a torrent. The water shot from the tank and sent everyone flying: the Lord Mayor, the aldermen, the councillors, the planners in their special bowler hats all tumbled against each other like a row of falling dominoes. The Lord Mayor's tri-cornered hat sailed swiftly down the town hall steps and the water gushed and roared out into the surrounding streets. In spite of their suggestion of a sympathetic element it showed no interest in Water Street or the river but raced eastwards, along Dale Street and out along London Road, tumbling and splashing, and sweeping all the rubbish along with it until it found itself racing down the East Lancashire Road and eventually lapped against the crumbly brick walls and red sandstone of the little villages and hamlets of vegetable Lancashire.

The planners and the councillors soon realised that when they opened the tap they had not properly calculated the force of pressure behind the Overspill. There was talk, that grew in volume as the Sixties started, of all those things such as Facilities for Youth that they had forgotten to think about in their enthusiasm for the idea – in the days when they first began to slap the inventor on the back until he was black and blue. All the armchair critics like Uncle Dermot said that it was always like this with any new idea and have you noticed, he said, that no-one ever knows where these ideas come from. And it is true that when the councillors and the aldermen and the planners looked at each other they realised that no-one could remember the name of the inventor.

But the Overspill raced on with such vigour and with such an unstoppable volume of water that Felix's father became a statistic. The young headmaster found himself in charge of the largest junior school in the British Isles. This caused a meeting of the Bishop and Monsignors of the Diocese. They sat around a long polished table in a gloomy room looked down on by a blue and white statue of the Virgin Mary who seemed to be saying to them, in spite of her butter-wouldn't-melt appearance: a nice mess you've got us into here. No-one knew what to do except to build new reservoirs to catch the Overspill and one by one the villages and hamlets stopped growing potatoes and turnips so that the fields could be concreted over for houses and schools and new churches and Facilities for Youth.

Because it was now the Sixties, the school (with its flapping doors with porthole windows and the smell of old tealeaves and disinfectant and stale sweat) soon began to start an overspill all of its own. Although the architects and builders had only just left, water seeped through the roof. One morning the young headmaster was forced to strap plastic buckets to the seat of his BSA motorbike to help to catch the drips when he got to work.

Eventually, everyone got used to the idea of Overspill, the way people always get used to ideas, whether or not they are good or bad. The people who lived in the new reservations were sometimes sad about the streets and squares they had left behind but no-one thought to ask them about this. Sometimes they remembered the corner pubs where the fat-bellied men in white shirts would gather on summer Saturday nights to quarrel, and jabber, and blather and waffle in the night air after chucking-out time.

Another new idea, one that Felix's father found much more sympathetic than bursting classrooms and dripping roofs and vexatious clergy, was to teach the little boys and girls of the Overspill foreign languages, starting with French. That was the night that Felix's father came home from work – for Felix lived in a family where everyone came home from school at night – with a little round cardboard badge that he had made for himself. It was the sort of badge that was used to make labels for stewards and judges on school sports days, a white disc edged with silver on whose blank surface you could write what you wished.

At tea-time, his father took his place at the head of the table wearing his new badge on which he had written in big black capital letters:

*MOI, JE SUIS DE LA CLASSE OUVRIÈRE!*

## 44. FUNNY HA-HA

IN THE CITY there were always jokes and when there were jokes, Uncle Dermot had usually heard them. He was not addicted solely to his own jokes and, like any conscientious connoisseur, was glad to acknowledge the distinction of others in the field. When he came to tea on special Saturdays or at Christmas – whether it was that he was tired out by work or by the journey which involved changing halfway from the green city buses to the red Ribble ones – he was always tired and would sometimes ask for *The Liverpool Echo* before closing his eyes on the comfortable sofa and falling asleep. If he started to snore, his wife and daughter would begin conversations to divert attention but that could not stop Felix and his brother and sister, whenever this happened, going behind the sofa to giggle.

It was generally the prospect of food or a glass of sherry that made Uncle Dermot sit up again and start telling jokes. When the talk came round to the fat Monsignor whose autocratic ways and peculiar sermons had created much stir in the parish, Uncle Dermot couldn't wait to recount the story of the wag who had declared, in the smoke and swirl and glass-clatter of the parish club: 'Who will rid me of this corpulent priest?'

## 45. A SHORT CHAPTER
## ABOUT LOVE

FELIX SAT ON A public bench in a wasteland of concrete flagstones in a provincial city. He was waiting, as he had so often waited. For love is about expectation – will she, won't she, was that her footstep on the stair, shall he be there, shall we be able to meet, shall we get away, shall this last for ever? Lovers waste so little time on the present moment in spite of all the urgings of the poets.

The wind blew a few scraps of paper and dead leaves across the open space. The sky was dull and heavy. And then a form, a shape, a way of moving, materialised in the distance. It was no longer the same landscape.

## 46. THE POETS

WHETHER THE POETS have been right or wrong, whether they have put their finger on what love is...

'Well, you know my views on the subject.'

'We certainly do, Trish.'

Whether they have led or followed the dance of love is an imponderable. Thomas Love Peacock mocked the sleepless nights of the tormented literary lover 'the ordinary effect of love, according to some amatory poets, who seem to have composed their whining ditties for the benevolent purpose of bestowing on others that gentle slumber of which they so pathetically lament the privation'. Yet Mr P himself was no stranger to the concept that formed his middle name. To speak directly the simplest words in the language, the ones that are simple even in the dead languages (*amo, amas, amat*) is not always easy. Our words come with all sorts of baggage (a memo to Monsieur de Saussure), crusted like a barnacled pot hauled from the sea with the accretion of other people's patter, those who have been this way before us, trying out the words and gestures, seeing if they can get it right. The words that have been said over and over keep needing to be said again, halting and tentative, as if they were being pronounced for the first time, which – for the pair in question – is exactly what is happening. But there's always a bit of poetry hanging around somewhere. Even the poets will tell you that. Take Sir Philip Sidney – a smooth-talking lover if ever there was one. He admits to consulting previous poetic form before placing a bet on his new love: 'Oft turning others' leaves, to see if thence would flow/Some fresh and fruitful showers upon my sunburn'd brain.' In the end he comes to the right conclusion (but poets never practise what they preach) that it's better to come right out with it than to hide behind the words of dead poets.

*Fool, said my Muse to me, look in thy heart, and write.*

# 47. THE PATCHWORK QUILT

A COUNTRY, a nation-state, likes to think of itself as a seamless quilt-cover in deep navy blue (brush off that fleck of white thread, lick your finger and erase that tiny fragment of unrinsed soap-powder) whereas it is a patchwork quilt, a brilliant stitching together of vivid bits and pieces. Not all squares are the same. Some are larger than others. Some are made of richer material. Some are neat and square. Others are awkward and asymmetrical. Some are discreet, like the unsmiling *bourgeois*, in a grey overcoat and black homburg, entering (in an expensive neighbourhood) the city park through a locked gate, with a small black dog at the end of his leash. Others are bright and vulgar like the shouting traders in a street-market. Some are very worn indeed and seem only just suitable enough to earn their place. But perhaps they make a contrast, make the expensive squares just that little more resplendent.

The politicians, who desire to tidy everything up, to create order-and-stability, to legislate against crooked and uneven shapes, have always been in love with the idea of a seamless, monochrome quilt thrown over the fat belly and protruding toes of the sleeping *bourgeois*. We are English. We are Germans. We are Greeks.

In the city of Thessaloniki a lexicographer has been instructed by a judge to remove a word from his dictionary. He has told his fellow-Greeks the meaning of a word whose meaning they know so well they wish to have it deleted. They wish to pretend that it does not exist. They consider it a stain on the freshly-laundered, freshly-ironed quilt. If one scratches out a word, if one puts down poison, if one sets a trap, if one closes the garden gate very tightly, the offence will not come in. Unfortunately, this is not how words work. They are as bad as ideas for they cannot be removed by any cleansing agent or killed off by any proprietary brand of poison, or aerosol spray. They are resistant to all known forms of sterilisation, of antibiotic. Like cheeky, scampering, laughing mice they scurry away behind the skirting board and run up and down under the floorboards squeaking: 'Catch me if you can!' The dictators, and the religious leaders, and the newspaper columnists have done their best but they have found that the more you try to eliminate a word or an idea, the more determined it seems to pop up, making rude faces, and sending out peals of defiant laughter.

When the football fans from Athens go to see a match with their rivals in Thessaloniki – and if by half time they are two goals down – they begin to taunt the Northeners with a chant: *Bu...Bu...Bulgarians! Bu...Bu...Bulgarians*! The Northeners are mad because they are Greeks and they thump their feet and chant: *Al...Al...Albanians! Al...Al...Albanians*! The metropolitan boys, with their All-Athens scarves waving like the distracted veils of a heroine of Greek tragedy, scream back their retaliatory chant at the PAOK fans because they too are Greeks. The lexicographer carefully makes a note in his card index. In his numbered list of definitions he enters the fact that on hot nights in Thessaloniki the southerners taunt the northerners with the accusation that they are no more than Bulgarians. They consider this the highest insult whereas the true insult is to the real Bulgarians. They are the ones who should be taking offence. They are the ones who should be dialling up in Yellow Pages whomever it is who issues late-night *fatwas*.

But words are not innocent and neither are lexicographers. The dictionary maker may be making a point as well as making a dictionary. He may be saying: this is very interesting. Someone recognises that the real quilt under the monochrome version has all sorts of colours and shapes, that worlds are made up of all sorts of bits and pieces. They may be football fans but they are also anthropologists, political scientists, philosophers in their way, who realise that no garment is ever seamless. The dictionary-maker – whose job it is to say how things are in the world of words – wants to tell the truth, to say that the cat of language has been let out of the bag and you may chase him all night around the streets of Thessaloniki but you won't get him in again now.

But the politicians and the judges and the newspaper columnists have other ideas. They think they can catch the cat and so they start a chase around the moonlit streets. They come clattering along the harbourfront and up the side alleys where surprised late-night drinkers of amber Metaxa and bitter black coffee look up startled when asked: 'Have you seen that black cat? Which way did it go?' They shrug their shoulders but the cat-chasers are already off.

All night long, down wide thoroughfares, across dark squares, and up narrow alleys the politicians and the judges and the columnists go chasing the elusive black cat of a word that they will never find. For the black cat has found a hiding place on a rusty old tramp steamer in the harbour where an old man in a dirty vest is feeding him with scraps of fish-heads thrown out of the galley by a Bulgarian cook with a passion for fish-soup.

# 48. THE DANCE

IT IS SUNDAY morning in the early autumn after the tourists have gone and when the fresh figs are turning from firm green into a squashy but succulent inner pulp. The sun is shining through the leaves of the trees which surround the dusty children's playground. The band has taken up position. The dance of the *sardana* is about to begin. Slowly, without the flashiness and whirl of other Mediterranean dances, the local people in their ordinary clothes gather for the dance. In other playgrounds and public spaces along the Rugged Coast this morning other dancers are taking up position. The band strikes up. The music is high and abrupt. At the end of the front row of chairs (where men in blue blazers are blowing into their instruments) the coolest musician of all, in dark shades, his body motionless, his face without expression, blows into the short, shrill pipe, the *flabiol* while, with his other hand, he taps the tiny *tambori*.

The dancers form rings, small at first, but growing larger all the time as another person slips into the chain. They lift their joined hands high into the air, composing a frieze of the kind one might see on an Attic vase of red and black. Their steps are slow but probably not easy. No outsider could risk joining in for these steps are prescribed and taught, handed down the generations. Without smiles or jollity or whoops or shouts, the solemn faces are intent on their slow dance, gentle, with a homely grace. The dance of Catalunya, the dance of a people who consider that a circle of hands in a dusty park on an October morning encloses something more than music and movement, something that, between themselves, needs no defining. Their serious steps, their raised hands, are lifted towards something. Shall we call it love?

'Let the games be played in Gaelic,' sneered MacNeice in another *Autumn Journal*: 'Put up what flag you like, it is too late/To save your soul with bunting.' Yes, yes, the last refuge of the scoundrel. But we must love something other than ourselves, our little purposes and private *amours*, the *petit bonheur* that sweetens a bitter day, the taste of a fig on a sunny wall, a snatch of music.

How to stop love turning into hate. How to dance the communal dance under the bright regional flag, holding one's neighbour's hands high, without coldness towards the other faces, to the people who do not know the steps of the dance, who cannot step forward and silently enter the ring, becoming one-in-many, part of the frieze.

The music goes on, the drummer beats his tiny drum, the rings dilate in the dusty playground in Catalunya.

# 49. PRIAPUS

HERE IS A canvas of Nicholas Poussin. *A Bacchanalian Revel Before a Herm of Pan.* This is a dance of sorts but there are no glum, intent faces here. This is love of the carnal sort, sexual love, what the English tabloid newspapers call 'bonking'.

'About time, too.'

'I'm sorry?'

'Have some regard for the marketing people. You put out a book with a title like this and it creates certain expectations. The punters are obviously going to want some action.'

'For a minute, Ted, I thought you were going to say: nudge, nudge.'

'You may mock, old son, but if we're going to turn you into a profit centre (book tours, literary festivals, puff slots on the breakfast show, celebrity profiles in the broadsheets) you are going to have to change your attitude. You are a product, a marketing opportunity. And don't give me any of that stuff about artistic integrity. Show me a writer who isn't interested in money.'

'Have you finished?'

'For the time being.'

To separate physical love from the other sorts which we call – because we can't think of a better word – Platonic is madness, I agree. The Puritans, who were often right-but-wrong, have done a lot of damage. Let's take another look at Poussin's bacchanale. There's a statue of Pan in the background, horned and garlanded, a grin as wide as the Mersey Tunnel, and *definitely* no underpants. The beautiful girls are revealing what used to be called their charms and the boys ditto. A naked youth has got his head deep in the fountain which (I'm jumping to conclusions here) is full of wine. This is not an event for the just-mineral-water-for-me brigade. Priapus, not to put too fine a point on it, is an old goat, big-bearded, lusty (I'm sorry, Trish, but the girls don't look to me as though they have any objection) tanned and with a goat's posterior. One of the girls is *very* enthusiastic, swinging a wine jug with one hand and groping goat-features's head with the other. In short, everyone is swinging. This is sexual love without the downside, the diseases, the wreckage, the consequences, the HIV. It's a painting in the National Gallery for God's sake.

'My point is, why aren't we getting anything sexier than this in your little pocket-epic?'

'Ted, I'm about to explain.'

And the explanation is simple. Just as we don't know what to do about silence, how to live with it, how to use it, how to listen to it, so we are losing touch with intimacy. Bacchanalia aside, sexual love is a fairly intimate affair, I think you'd agree. Opening the door, pulling up the blind on the two-way mirror, letting the cameras roll, gives us all an eyeful (look at the average night's TV) but does it get us anywhere? Perhaps we have become a nation of voyeurs, of people in dirty macs, Peeping Toms, salivating over the advance puff in the TV mag that tells us what to expect (know what I mean?) in the evening's viewing. What I'm suggesting is that we should spend a little more time getting on with it than getting off on it, if you read me. Most sex-scenes in literature are awful. Have you ever read such tosh as *Lady Chatterley's Lover*? Your bookshop seeker after highbrow smut has plenty to choose from. There's a glut of it. Which means that I am not required to add to the pile.

...*ohne die Liebe/Wäre die Welt nicht die Welt*. How could we not agree with Goethe that a world without love is no world at all. And Goethe was no Puritan. No, sir.

And neither am I.

## 50. OF TINY FEET

FREEDOM FROM OR freedom to. We ought to prefer the latter to the former but that's not how things work. Freedom starts to matter usually at the point where it is about to be taken away. It's something people are prepared to die for, which might seem a contradiction, for the grave offers few opportunities for the exercise of liberty. There are those, of course, who are not in love with freedom, like that dictator looking down into the square on his marching cohorts, resenting the freedom of the bird. Authoritarians, disciplinarians, people who love bossing other people around, stamping on outbreaks of freedom as if they were scuttling beetles on a paved walkway. These people love not freedom but coercion. They love to feel their power. From somewhere they derive the notion that they have a right to be in charge, to lay down the law, to argue that a free conscience is disloyalty. There are very many people like this. Moreover, they are abetted by a very curious set of people, the ones who love to have their freedom taken away, who struggle to the front of the queue and shout: 'Here, have mine, I don't need it anyway, it's no use, it's more trouble than it's worth, and while you're at it why don't you take his and hers away? I can't see that they need it either. People make too much of a fuss about freedom. I wish they'd simply shut up.'

Felix walked across the vast city of Kunming, through markets selling every kind of living thing (snakes, rodents, parrots, dogs and cats), past stalls selling hot and spicy noodles, past tea-houses, down dusty streets, and across wider ones full of long articulated buses and throngs of silent bicycles. Waiting at traffic lights, Felix looked down at the elderly woman in a padded, embroidered jacket, and saw that her tiny feet in brocaded slippers were far tinier than any normal foot should be. Her feet, as a young woman, had had their freedom taken away by someone in authority. They had been squeezed and cramped and shackled until they agreed not to grow any more. For the rest of her life this woman would walk with difficulty because someone had decided that her freedom must be torn up and used to line the inside of his ego. And many others had come forward to help in the business of curbing those licentious toes, arguing that this had Always Been Done, and praising tradition and the virtues of obedience.

After a long walk, Felix reached the university where students sat on the grass reading books (as students do in places other than Yunnan province). He was taken to visit six students of English who sat on their bunks learning lists of etymologies, which is a boring thing to do. When Felix arrived they sprang down from their bunks (they seemed to live in what looked like an abandoned barracks) and told him all about themselves, how six young men lived in one room with one desk, how they wanted to be translators or tourist guides, how they dreaded being told to become teachers which would mean going to some bleak provincial place where they knew no-one and where the pay was awful. Felix thought there was something wrong in a country that made young men and women dread to become teachers, that gave them no choice in the matter. He was free to wander in the city, to take a bowl of noodles in a crowded restaurant, to go on, to pack his bags in the morning, to discover a new place. But it is always easier to see how other people's liberties are taken away and to overlook the same thing in one's own country.

Later, Felix would accept the kindness of a man in the noodle shop who helped him to order, who pointed to the stack of re-used wooden chopsticks and smiled when Felix produced his own from an inside pocket. The man was a teacher too but he had been denounced during the madness of the revolution as a backward element. He had been put in jail. Who put you there, asked Felix. The man smiled a cracked, old man's smile, as if this were the funniest thing that had ever happened to him.

'The citizens.'

# 51. THE SEA, THE SEA

ON HOT SUMMER Saturdays the family would get into the car and drive north along the coast, leaving behind the sewer outlets and the polluted beach with its litter of driftwood, plastic bottles, grease-balls, vestigial seaweed, bits of rope, and electric light bulbs. Parking the car in the pine woods, they would walk, carrying the picnic basket, through the sandy dunes with their spiky outcrops of marram grass. Sometimes they stopped along the route to pick blackberries, dusted with a film of blown sand.

Felix watched his father striding ahead, mounting the last row of dunes, and looking on the sea where he would at last cry: '*Thalassa! Thalassa!*' Felix could never remember which Greek had reported this cry (Herodotus? Thucydides? Xenophon?) or whether it was the Persians, or the Spartans, or the Greeks, seeing the blue ocean after a long march. His father would know, as he seemed to know most things. He had learned his Latin and Greek in a bleak Lancashire seminary (for he had gone further than Felix, marking his paper with an enormous YES). There the little boys learning their *amo, amas, amat* sometimes felt hungry. Later, he had gone to Rome where the sun shone and there was wine on the refectory table and a new language to learn. *Se non è vero è ben trovato!* he would mutter at some of Uncle Dermot's stories. And to while away the time on a troopship to India he had learned Urdu. Languages, words, phrases, quotations that were funny and curious delighted his father. Browning's 'Soliloquy in a Spanish Cloister' with its clerical small-talk ('Not a plenteous cork-crop, I fear') was often on his lips; titles of books (*Every Man His Own Farrier*); the wireless announcer in Ireland *circa* 1934 ('And now Mr Murphy will give a talk on potatoes') were all grist to his language-delighting mill. And Matthew Arnold's scholar-gypsy, looking across the Cumnor hills to Oxford where the lit-up colleges sent out their semaphore of bright exclusion, spoke to him – in another line that would often be declaimed: 'The line of festal light in Christchurch Hall.'

The dull Irish Sea, the tide far out, the flat sand firm and golden, a few pieces of bleached driftwood scattered here and there. The cry of gulls. *Thalassa! Thalassa!*

# 52. THE HAMMOCK

UNCLE DENIS WAS the practical one of his many brothers. The family lived above the barber's shop where Grandfather Felix shaved the chins of the city's working men, lecturing them about Socialism as they sat on the long, polished bench (on which his children, after hours, would play Grand National, shooting white paper horses along its smooth surface). His captive audience would be treated to excerpts and facts and figures from Robert Blatchford's *Clarion* which he kept permanently folded on top of the sterilised cabinet. Felix never knew his grandfather, who died when his boys were small, but his grandmother survived, another joking lady who might be considered to have had, in a hard life, relatively little to joke about. But in a city where jokes hopped about like pigeons in the square she couldn't stay immune. She died when he, too, was small, but he remembered her biscuit barrel from which he would be rewarded and her fondness for rolling up a newspaper and tapping it rhythmically on his head as she sang:

*Felix, Felix,*
*Boil his head.*
*Make it into gingerbread!*

Upstairs, Uncle Denis was said to keep a pot of glue permanently by the fire, for he was always making things. Surrounded by so many brothers and sisters who were good at words he decided to be good with his hands. He was restless and active, constantly thinking up things to make or repair. Once, he made a hammock out of a piece of

139

discarded canvas someone had found down by the docks. He cut and trimmed and stitched and glued and hammered and bound until the hammock was finished. Uncle Denis loved a job well done and this was a beautiful job. Everyone came to see the hammock strung up between two posts. Uncle Denis climbed in to the hammock and put his hands behind his head like a lazy passenger on a cruise liner drifting through the tropics. It was just the sort of comfortable position that one could imagine oneself luxuriating in for a very long time. That is, if one was not Uncle Denis, if one knew how to relax and to luxuriate and to savour what the Italians call the *dolce far niente*.

For thirty seconds, everyone watched Uncle Denis doing his impersonation of a comfortable idler. Then up he jumped, scuttling upstairs to his glue-pot and his next project.

He would not have lasted long in the Forest of Morroiz.

## 53. THE LOVE OF TRUTH

WHAT IS TRUTH, said jesting Pilate, and stayed not for an answer. Francis Bacon. Perhaps there couldn't be an answer. Some things are too big to be shrunk down to the dimensions of our little definitions. Philip Larkin took refuge in alliteration. *In this way I spent youth,/Tracing the trite untransferable/Truss-advertisement, truth.* He was talking, not of the truth of the seminar room, the punctilious monograph, the orotund philosophical declaration, but the truth of life, the Holy Grail that will tell us: this is what it is all for, this is what you must do. No wonder he was a bit cynical.

It starts by being clear as mud, then we start to get bright ideas, then it's clear as mud again. Priests, politicians, preachers of every stripe, have a head start. The carved rim of that pulpit (always raised up above us) that they grip with the hand that isn't raised to punch the air or slam down the good book, is like a roped barrier, a police tape, a line in the sand. If they were standing down here with us they wouldn't be so cocksure, so flipping smug.

Truth's out of fashion. Or it's whatever you fancy. Perhaps it's where you come from, the gathering ball of memories, stories, jokes, echoes, fragments that rolls on whether you like it or not. Felix's father would talk about Truth. He tried to find out, at the time, the Truth about the Spanish Civil War but it couldn't be done. Not by reading both sides, adding up and subtracting, saying yes and yes but, balancing both brass pans of the scale. Truth is elusive, it never lives up to its Idea, but we can't be without it. Isn't it a bit like love?

# 54. IT DOESN'T LAST

WHENEVER WE OVERHEAR the complaints of lovers it is always the same old tune. It's as if they feel they have to pay a tax on love. This is so good someone must be paying for it – which they generally do. One night of pleasure. One night when the whole world can go hang, when everything that led up to this seems like a mere prelude, a clearing of the ground. Don't hand me the *Which?* magazine. Don't educate me about the alternatives. This is it. This is now. Don't prattle about the Millennium, the century's end, the century's beginning, the mystic pile-up of numbers, the changing of the clocks. This is for now. This is for real.

And then, the morning after, the whingeing starts.

The sixteenth century poets were good at this sort of thing. Even when they were stealing the clothes of others they made it sound convincing. Poor old Sir Thomas Wyatt:

> *They flee from me that sometyme did me seke*
> *With naked fote stalking in my chambre*

That's not very nice, is it? Trish won't like that, the woman as a shy gazelle eating acorns from the lover's hand. Then, as soon as she's had enough, the frail thing has turned into a wild beast. The woman has become a demon again, a witch, putting a curse on the man who trusted her. But poor Sir Tom, even as he moans, remembers. He can't get out of his head the memory of that one time, that this-is-for-now, that 'ons in speciall' when she came to him, barefooted in his chamber: *When her lose gowne from her shoulders did fall.* He remembers her nakedness, her tenderness, her kiss and its

142

accompanying query: *dere hert, howe like you this?* It was no dream, he assures us, *I laye brode waking.* The lovers in their private chamber are in and out of a dream. Life is not normally like this but this is more real than anything else has ever been. Sir Tom has been there, to the place that, in the strange cosmology of lovers seems, at the time, the only planet (*ohne die Liebe/Wäre die Welt nicht die Welt*). Sexual passion, like Art, is not an escape from life it is life, a tasting of the hyper-real. And, in the dusty old knight's dusty old manuscript with its antique spelling, the electricity crackles.

And then, of course, he starts to moan, to wish that she, too, now has cause to moan, who left him for no better reason than the tilt of another courtier's cap. But that doesn't matter. In this sort of poem you're meant to moan. It's the price you pay for stanza two. For the shock of recognition. For the knowledge that you have been there too, in the dark chamber, where a silk gown rustles and the horses of the night obligingly slow to a pleasant canter.

*Dere hert, howe like you this?*

# 55. OF FIRE

FELIX FOLLOWED HIS father along the street between the glass-and-concrete church and the glass-and-concrete school. It was quiet as they unlocked the swing doors and pushed through into the reeking corridors and unlocked the headmaster's office with a metallic clatter of keys and snapping locks. His father looked around his office, at the pegboard with its coloured pegs representing teachers and subjects, at the machine for binding cellophane covers for library books, at the menacingly silent cane in the corner against the wall, at the papers and trays, and clutter. It was cold crisp Easter and the cries and shouts and thundering feet were all on holiday.

'We'd better go and see O'Halloran,' said his father.

They walked the whole length of a corridor, and then another, and then another, until they came to a door with a round porthole through which his father looked. They went in and down a short flight of steps to another door below ground. Felix had been reading *David Copperfield* in an edition with pictures and, when the door of the boiler-room opened, to his astonishment he found himself face to face with Uriah Heep. O'Halloran, the school caretaker had been sitting at a little table with two black-faced coalmen. They were drinking tea from a flask and dipping their hands into a greaseproofed loaf-wrapper in which was spread a pile of sandwiches. Felix noticed that one of the coalmen had left a black thumbprint in the soft white texture of an abandoned sandwich. They had opened the door of the furnace to warm their hands.

When he saw the headmaster, O'Halloran leaped up and began to rub his hands together and address the newcomer as 'Sir'. The coalmen continued to sip their mugs of tea and watch the caretaker's antics with a quiet complacency. O'Halloran was a mystery. It was said that he had once been a seminarian. In another version he had been an undertaker's assistant. His pale, drawn features and his obsequious manner would have made the latter an obvious speculation. It was rumoured that he was a scholar but he gave little away in conversation, taking refuge behind a multiplicity of compliant gestures and formulaic phrases. He put his hand on Felix's shoulder and steered him towards the open furnace door which was frighteningly hot on the boy's cheeks and made him lift his hand to shield his eyes. The coalmen laughed and told him not to put his hand into the fire. O'Halloran looked at the headmaster and then across at the coalmen with a glance of sharp disapproval. Felix drew back from the furnace and his father said it was time to go. They left O'Halloran, bowing and scraping, in their wake.

On the fringe of a Midlands city, beyond the clusters of superstores, and the sprawl of miscellaneous trading estates, the railings and well-kept lawns of the crematorium came into view. From the car park one set of mourners departing wordlessly met another set of mourners arriving. Some faces were pale and silenced by grief, others were jaunty as if this were all a bit of a lark, as if Jack would have found all this comical, the old sod. There was a waiting room with a scatter of women's magazines as if it were a dentist's surgery. Most preferred to stand outside in the cold, trying to be cheerful, hoping it would soon be over, dreading the banality of the piped music, and the swishing curtain, and the po-faced undertaker's men. There was a sense that, somehow, more people ought to have been here. What did one say on such occasions? What did one do? What would he/she have wanted?

It was over in minutes. The next contingent was waiting outside. More cars were arriving at the carpark. Another box was slid into the municipal furnace. Someone caught himself looking up to see if a plume of smoke was visible against the thick, pasty sky.

# 56. THE APRON

FELIX HELPED HIS father to trundle the wardrobe out into the street and into the back of the car. They drove off towards the south, towards the start of the docks, where cranes and grain silos and clear fences rather than the old high walls of the Victorian docks allowed one to see the container ships with decks piled high with boxes. These boats were more like a lorry than a ship of the kind Felix had once drawn at school with black crayons for the angled smokestack and white for the row of portholes in the hull.

The woman who had seen the card in the post office stood on her doorstep in Knowsley Road, her arms on her hips, a fierce matriarch. She eyed the piece of furniture sceptically, watched the father and son manhandle it into her hallway, offering no help, stroking it with one hand to take the measure of her bargain, grudgingly disappearing into the kitchen to fetch a pair of crumbled banknotes.

As he slammed shut the rear door of the car, Felix saw his father straighten up and look down the road. After a minute or two of silence, he pointed towards a public house with a swinging sign on which a red and black funnelled Cunard liner was painted. He told Felix how his father had been in the habit, after the shop was shut, of tucking his white barber's apron into his belt and heading off for a pint here. Father and son looked across the road silently. A double-decker bus drew up in front of them, blocking the view. They turned away and got back in the car. The bus moved on. A brewer's lorry stood outside the pub, rolling silver-grey barrels down into the cellar, unloading crates with a repeated crash.

# 57. THE PITY OF IT

IT HAS BEEN argued that love is an affair of equals. No dominant males and submissive females, no testosterone swagger and simpering shyness, but two people in love, giving and taking in equal measure. All fine and dandy, but in the republic of love not all citizens are equal. In the pursuit of love one would not always start from here. A question. Can love sometimes be a form of pity?

Or even a form of forgetting? A way of saying that all is forgiven: the bad behaviour, the injustice, the indictable offences. Love as a healing balm, an application over old wounds. More than this, a way of saying that one understands, that bad behaviour may proceed from invisible hurts and wounds, that love might find a way to soften the pain, that nothing is served by tenderly nursing a sense of grievance as if it were a frail and sickly plant that should simply be allowed to die. Let go of hate, let go of resentment, tear up the charge sheet and open the cell door. Let love in.

Perseus, flying back from his encounter with the Gorgon Medusa, one of whose glances would turn a man or woman to stone, flying back with Medusa's head in a travel-bag, its ugly hair-tangle of vile serpents still capable of petrifying anyone who got in its way, made a stopover in Philistia. Feeling pleased with himself at having outwitted the Gorgon (the reflection in a shield rather than a death-inducing gander guiding him to his object), Perseus looked down on the beautiful Andromeda, naked except for a few glittering jewels, bound cruelly to a rock to await her fate: to be consumed by a sea monster. Perseus took pity on Andromeda. And his pity turned to love.

The sins of the fathers. Andromeda's mother had boasted that she and her daughter were more beautiful than the Nereids. Probably true, but the lovely sea-nymphs complained to their boss, Poseidon, who agreed that such an insult demanded that Philistia be punished with a flood and a devouring sea-monster. The oracles (typically) demanded that her father sacrifice his daughter to the monster, that she be offered up, bound to a rock to await the snapping teeth of the sea-beast, so that the oldies could be put in the clear. When Perseus touched down they promised (with forked tongue because they were first and foremost concerned with themselves) that he could have Andromeda as his bride if he killed the monster. That was the easy part, for he was later forced to defend himself from their trickery, turn a whole lot more folk to stone by exposing the contents of his flight-bag, and flee with his beautiful bride to the lovely Aegean island of Serifos which you will have seen in the brochures.

As well as pity there is gratitude, which may have entered into Andromeda's estimate of her new love (though no-one seems to have consulted her feelings about the match). So perhaps love is not equal after all. Or, from another point of view, there is so much give and take that no-one knows how to reconcile the account. But, unlike the stuff that accountants deal in, there is always enough love to go round. It grows on trees and you can spend as much as you like – though it's odd how many people forget this.

# 58. A MORAL

ONE CAN HEAR the moralists shuffling uneasily in their pulpits. All this talk of love. All this talk of passion, of the present moment, of seizing the day, of rapture rather than repentance, of exalted pleasure rather than duty, of today rather than tomorrow. What's in this for the Puritan who still stalks the undergrowth of the Western mind with a glittering eye of judgement and a cold heart?

In a world where so little is now left to chance, where rules and regulations proliferate, where the vacuous patter of salesmen and the clatter of cash-tills and the crackle of credit-card vouchers drown out the silence, where life can sometimes seem little more than a shopping opportunity, where the people who run theatres and museums and galleries have come to sound like double-glazing salesmen, where politics is a servile pursuit of what is marketable – then a little madness, a little unreasonable passion, might not come amiss, might be considered a Good Thing. And if it means pain and suffering, if it tears the heart in two, if it makes us ask: should this have happened? couldn't we have chosen a quieter life? well, so be it. That's the nature of love. And a world without love, as Goethe put it, is no world at all.

Yes, it's Dionysian. Yes, it's one in the eye for the Apollonian sages with their crystal logic and cold calculation, their soldered microchips. But a new century is being revved up outside. It has seen what happens when the Grand Planners are let loose. It has seen so many corpses, so many rounded up and jabbed with electric prods in cold corridors, so many drowned in carpet bombs and napalm and atomic fallout, so much that has flowed from Ideas.

Here's another one. A Big Idea to put in your Millennium Dome, lit by laser-beams, nodded at by politicians on the opening morning. A Big Idea that's a Small Idea: start by loving yourself, scraping out all that detritus of hate and filling it up again with its opposite. Then spread it around and see what happens.

Tell that to the birds, sunshine.

# 59. THE END

AFTER THE FURTHER adventures of the lovers. After the madness of Tristan and the despair of Iseut. After being forced to live apart from her in exile in Brittany with Iseut of the White Hands, Tristan got himself into another scrape and was wounded by a poisoned lance.

No doctor could cure his wound and Tristan knew that the only person in the world who had the power to draw the poison was Iseut the Fair. He sent a messenger across the sea to summon Iseut and gave instructions that the ship must bear white sails if it was bringing back his love and black sails if she would not come. Iseut lost no time in putting to sea but the ship was delayed, first by a storm, and then, as the Brittany coast appeared, by a sudden becalming. And Tristan was dying. Perhaps it was no more than justice that a love that had contained so many deceptions and crafty stratagems, so many secret meetings, false reports, deceiving reflections in moonlit water, bogus confessions, and cease-less two-timing, would result in love's treachery being the agent of their undoing.

Iseut of the White Hands, in no way relishing the arrival of her namesake and rival, heard the story of the sails. And so, when the dying Tristan asked what sails were flapping weakly on the becalmed vessel of the ship that was visible from the coast, she replied in a sugary voice: 'They are black, my love.' And Tristan turned away in despair – even though now the wind was getting up and Iseut the Fair's spirits were rising. Convinced that nothing would now save him he turned his face to the wall and his heart cracked in two and he died. When Iseut's boat came in, and when she discovered the cause of the weeping and wailing in the streets, as if a Princess had died, she too began to howl. Seeking out the corpse of Tristan, she threw herself on it. There had been too much love, too much passion, in their life since they swallowed the love-potion and she could not take any more. And so she joined him in death.

Standing outside the tall building, lit with sodium strips on a bleak winter afternoon, Felix paused. People poured in and out of Fazakerley, paying their tribute of flowers and unwanted grapes. Felix paused on the steps. He looked absently at the crowds, the purring taxis, the comings and the goings, but he was seeing none of it. He was thinking all the usual, predictable thoughts and coming to no conclusions.

It seemed always that he was walking away. It seemed that this was what he did best: making himself into an absence.

He drove out of the city, along the darkening, traffic-thickened streets, then through the tiled tunnel under the river, out across the flat counties of Cheshire and North Wales. Lorries with flapping loads roared along the dual carriageway as the sky grew dark. The city receded. The thoughts began to regroup and offer themselves up into new patterns. But he was not tempted by their glib conclusions, their tidying up of the mess, their raised, prefabricated sections, as he sped towards the gathering darkness of the West.

*Sub-arachnoid.* How his father would have appreciated that etymology, the spider of blood leaving its malign spoor on the sentient brain, leaving a strong fierce light in his eye, a strong grip that Felix had held firm and long before moving off, before becoming, yet again, an absence.

*Will you love me till I'm fifty dead?*
*Will you love me till I'm fifty dead?*

# Acknowledgements

The following sources were used for the Tristan and Iseut legend:

*Tristan in Brittany* (1929) translated by Dorothy L. Sayers

*The Romance of Tristan and the Tale of Tristan's Madness* (Harmondsworth, 1970) translated by Alan S. Fredrick

*The Romance of Tristan* (Oxford, 1994) translated by Renée L. Curtis

*Gottfried von Strassburg's Tristan with the Tristan of Thomas* (Harmondsworth, 1960) translated by Arthur Thomas Hatto

*Tristan et Iseut: Les poèmes français* (Paris, 1989) edited by Daniel Lacroix & Philippe Walter

# About the Author

Nicholas Murray has written biographies of Bruce Chatwin, Matthew Arnold, and Andrew Marvell, and has published a collection of poems, *Plausible Fictions*. His poems, essays and reviews have appeared in a wide range of newspapers and periodicals. Born and brought up in Liverpool, he now lives in London and the Welsh Marches. He recently completed a major biography of Aldous Huxley, which will be published in 2002.